# PLURALITIES

# PLURALITIES

## AVI SILVER

Atthis Arts

# PLURALITIES

Published by Atthis Arts, LLC
Detroit, Michigan
atthisarts.com

ISBN 978-1-961654-00-6

Library of Congress Control Number: 2023943284

For Anna, somewhere in time.

*i.*

Wait—rewind. I was still a girl back then, before the universes converged. Not a very good one, but I had the SHE stamp in blue ink right across my cheek, smudged to hell, not even convincing enough to pass for a birthmark. Maybe that should have been the first sign.

I was working a dead-end *she*-shaped job with a bunch of other *she*s with perfectly matte stamps and hair like Sunday brunch. We all smiled a lot. It made my jaw hurt. For six to eight hours a day, I touched strangers, rubbing lotion into their tired arms and spouting off ingredients like my voice box had come pre-recorded. They listened to me, and looked right at my eyes, and spent money because they were afraid their children didn't know anybody loved them.

On that last day, the manager pulled me outside of the shop for a private meeting. We sat together on one of the pieces of modern art masquerading as a bench. "Let's have a conversation!" she said, smiling.

"Sure!" I said, smiling.

"Great!" she said, smiling. "I couldn't help but notice that the last friend—" (We weren't allowed to call them customers.) "—whose arm you were massaging left in tears! Tell me about that!"

I have this habit of reading people's futures on their skin. Physical contact is like a wormhole, and back then, when I was still a girl, I thought this dead-end job would be a safe place to be an oracle. Maybe get some good discounts on foot lotion for my mom.

"Yeah," I said, smiling. "Her son's been missing for weeks. Presumed dead. But he's safe. He's coming home."

"How exciting!" she said, smiling. "That's so great that you learned something personal about your new friend to boost your sales drivers! High-five!"

She went in for the high-five like a particularly ambitious jack-in-the-box. I had told her a dozen times about the visions, but she never seemed to remember—which was probably why she looked so offended when I ducked away from her hand. Maybe that should have been the first sign.

Her nails tapped on the clipboard she carried around, right over the sticker that said *I'm Managing!* "Can I give you some feedback?"

"Sure!" I said, smiling. (We weren't allowed to say no to feedback.)

"When you create overly meaningful connections with friends, sometimes it can scare off potential friends who are just hoping to try out some skin care! Try to connect a little bit *less* in the future, that way you don't intimidate anyone!" she said, smiling.

This shouldn't have bothered me. We'd had this conversation too many times over the past year, and I'd learned to put in about a week of effort before I gave back in to the oracular tendencies. The premonitions weren't really something I could control, and the manager really seemed to like having this conversation with me. I figured being a denizen of retail hell was tough, and I didn't want to take it away from her by improving myself. I was a good employee. I was a good person. I wasn't smiling anymore.

Maybe that should have been the first sign.

"I just feel," I began, intruding on the pause that had gone a beat too long, "I just feel like the customers—"

"Friends," she corrected, smiling enough for the both of us. "The *friends we make along the way*."

"Okay," I tried again. Some kid was losing it on the other side of the mall fountain. I'd rubbed his mother's arm earlier; he was about to fall in. "I just feel like some of the *friends we make along the way* are sort of starved for contact, you know? I mean we're the only place in the mall that offers complimentary massages, and there are plenty of stores with better lotion, so—"

My manager's face changed then, a twitch up by the corner of her right eyelid, tugging at the SHE stamp on her cheek. It matched her lipstick: silken amaranth, undisturbed by forgetful fingers. The slope of her eyeliner curved in a cruel arch as her expression shifted from manufactured warmth to unfiltered disdain. I could have loved her for the honesty in that look.

*Splash!*

A scream from the other side of the fountain; adults clucking as they scooped the sopping child out of the water like the world's worst prize at a carnival fishing game. My manager only looked at me, taking a deep breath as she swallowed back down whatever bitter, tired thing it was she wanted to say. She crossed one long leg over the other, adjusting the clipboard in her lap.

"We're so lucky to work in such a welcoming environment, don't you think?" she asked, smiling.

"Yeah," I said. My ears rang with the sound of sobbing on the other side of the fountain, amplified by parental cooing and shushing.

"Not every place is like this, you know!" she insisted, smiling.

"Nope," I agreed.

"And corporate pays us such a good wage!" she said, smiling.

*It's the minimum wage,* I thought. *It's the minimum amount of money they can legally pay us.*

But I just stared at her, looking for the right thing to say. Looking for a reason not to make like the five-year-old across the way and pitch myself into the fountain. Looking for an in, an out, an escape plan for the past two years of my life.

Then she gave me one.

She reached out to touch my arm, to do her best imitation of a reassuring waitress at a local diner, but the millisecond after her acrylic nails made contact, it came rushing in like it always does:

*The clock on the laptop screen reads 3:07pm. It's April nineteenth. She's crossing off my name on the schedule and talking to the regional manager on the phone. She's crouched on the minifridge because the floor's covered in half-unloaded palettes of salt scrub and cuticle cream. "I don't know what happened," she's saying. "It was all so sudden, like some kind of a nervous breakdown! I mean, at least she turned in her t-shirt, but I don't really want to pass it onto anyone else. Such bad vibes!"*

"Hello? Earth to *She*?" she laughed, her sing-song voice gone tinny.

I reached into my pocket, pulling out my phone: *April 19th. 2:56pm*. I smiled wide enough to taste my fillings, mercurial and wild. I pulled off my branded t-shirt and dropped it onto her clipboard, so I was just sitting on the bench in my shitty gray bra. People stared as they walked by. My manager didn't know where to look.

*"I fucking hate this place,"* I said, smiling.

So I left.

*Meanwhile, among the neurons and nebulae . . .*

Prince Cornelius Flux leaves his homeworld in a rush of aubergine velvet and vetivert smoke, feeling the disapproving gaze of 11.6 billion subjects of varying species and political alignments. His exit shouldn't come as a shock; he's been openly discussing his plans for the past several weeks, in every place from the Robotics Parlors to the Lunar Nightclubs to the breakfast table.

"It's hard to explain," he says to a suitor on his last planetbound evening, watching the steady blink of her neural implant. Pretty. "Sometimes a man and his ship just need some time alone together. You know how the bots get when they feel neglected."

"But Your *Highness*," she replies, her face a portrait of dutiful concern as she rests a hand high on his thigh. Beside her, her neurally-linked service bot sings a sultry tune. "What about your family? What about your paramours?"

In the stifling air of the crowded music hall, the prince sees himself reflected in her eyes. The whole of him, contained, *constrained* by the limits of her dilating pupil.

"Haven't you thought about what *they* might want for you?"

By dawn, he breaks through the weight of the atmosphere.

The prince—no, not a prince anymore, the *rogue*—tugs the royal medal loose from his coat, his breath catching at the snap of thread. The pearled heirloom seems to glow in his palm, the ship's in-floor lighting reflecting the pale lavender of his skin. He grips it tighter, shakes his head to free the swirling antennae caught in his milky curls. Reminds himself, for the hundredth time, to claim the personality he so desperately wants.

He drops the glinting medal into his pilot chair's cup holder with a clang. It isn't his business if everyone decides to bristle over his leaving. If they had listened instead of brushing him off, he would have gladly explained himself. But they didn't. They never do.

So he sits now at the helm of his ship, a self-sustaining Bionic Organic Developmental Ylem unit that has shaped itself into a sturdy duochrome bachelor pad, bound for whatever hunk of rock looks hospitable enough to hold them both. Cornelius, the rogue—he doesn't intend on staying anywhere for too long. He'll dip his toes in the oceans that won't boil him, have a taste of the local delicacies that won't bite back, take a lover, duel a foe. Move on. That's the point, right?

"Still no signs of being followed, Bo?" he asks, wincing at the anxious flavor under his tongue.

The ship's overhead lights flutter a reassuring periwinkle before promptly shifting to an irritable pop of atomic tangerine. A low thrum sends tremors through the metal floorboards.

"I'm not being paranoid," the rogue responds sourly. "You know how my mothers are."

The bulbs spiral, good as an eye-roll, and the ship's upper paneling clunks off to the sides, widening the view from the cockpit window. As if any of the rogue's eyes have the capacity to see into deep space.

"Very helpful, smartass." The bot's always like this—nurturing by way of needling, its figurative heels dug in at every turn. Worst of all, it has a habit of almost always being right, which it uses as an excuse to nag its pilot into oblivion. Not that he's ungrateful—if Cornelius is daring to be honest with himself, this much-needed great escape was mostly Bo's idea in the first place.

It's a good thing, to go adventuring this way. Like when they were young, and the ship was still building itself around its sentient ylem core. It'll be healthy to have some time alone together. Why shouldn't it be?

"Alright," he mutters to himself, sighing out the doubt threatening to wormhole into his chest. "Let's get some tunes going before we face that sweet void, huh?" With a whir of acquiescence, the overhead lights go soft, and Bo puts on the latest release from the Radiator Vixens.

The rogue clicks his seat back and lolls his head back onto the curved rest as the cabin fills with atmospheric electropop. He didn't realize the ship had updated its sound system. "You're brilliant, Bo-sephine."

The intercom squawks at the name, indignant.

"Bo-stophales?" he tries, grinning.

Irritable static.

"Bo-nafide friend o' mine?" The alarm on the airlock blares, and the rogue's arms shoot up defensively. "Alright, alright! Just Bo. My cranky Bo."

He knocks playfully on the B.O.D.Y. unit's side paneling and the navigation screen flickers to life with a whine, lighting up with a map of the galaxy. The rogue rubs his hands together, leaning in to face his distant neighborhood. Worlds awaken like sparks of phosphorous, like crackling candy, like the hiss of acid rain at third summer's end. Some of the names he reads are familiar: longstanding trade partners, satellite embassies, labor lands, pleasure moons. But many of them mean little to him, or else are identified only with numbers and color ratings signifying their presence in the catalog and the extent of logged exploration.

The prince—no, the *rogue*—pulls off his velvet jacket, and Bo's grasping mechanisms whir as they hang it up. It is a quiet relief to free his neck and shoulders from the unexpected heaviness of his exit, from the lingering scent of his last hours on familiar soil. The set of eyes on his throat blink their scaled lids, adjusting as they briefly take in the heat signatures around them; Bo's ylem core burns a brilliant red, the cool walls deep violet, his own hand something in between. The cabin's air is pleasantly dry, the crisp remnants of his own breath cleaned and recycled through Bo's inner workings. He'd call it symbiotic, if it weren't for the strained frisson of energy strung between them like sputtering fluorescent light.

It hasn't always been like this.

Has it?

"Alright, baby." The rogue drums his fingers on the screen, feeling each pulse strike him low in the chest. Information about each world pops up beneath his touch, messages of warning and invitation alike. Nothing but possibility ahead. "Where to first?"

*ii.*

I sat at the bus stop outside the mall for what felt like five hours but was probably actually about thirty-two minutes before the bus came. It was one of those heinous little moments where you go charging at the bus like you've got something to prove in the fifth-grade fitness test, but then it drives off anyway, so you're stuck waiting for the next bus in your bra. So now people are gawking, and then the next bus is late by like three minutes, and you're unjustifiably furious with the driver even though it's not that big of a deal, but it *is* a big deal because their three minutes late is your thirty-two minutes on a dirty bench outside the mall, watching strangers enjoy the privacy of their cars and feeling like fucking Tantalus at the Subaru Summer Sales Event.

You know. One of those moments.

As a very recent fugitive of the service industry, I was doing my best not to be rude to the driver. Labor solidarity, etc. I dug for the fare in the tiny leather backpack my mom got me last Chanukah, cursing its bafflingly small compartments. Sure, I could fit in a wallet, a phone, a small notebook, maybe sunglasses if I decided to get over the amount of squinting I do, but the second even a little bit of bag garbage accumulated, it was all over. Takeout napkins, ticket stubs, receipts. Death by a thousand papercuts.

The driver cleared his throat as I scraped my fingers along the bottom of the bag. Usually the buses started moving the second the passengers stepped off the sidewalk—and honestly, with the three minute delay, it probably would have been better for the sake of the route—but this guy was real old school. He grunted, foot on the brake, not looking at me. Finally, the coins found my fingers. I dropped them into the bin and rubbed at my cheek, further maiming the smudged SHE stamp.

I'd barely taken a step when the voice rang out: "You can't ride this bus."

What?

"What?" I looked up and found myself eye-to-eye with a woman who looked like she'd spoken to one too many managers in her lifetime. Her SHE stamp was straight out of an ad for a high-end department store. She had her hand pressed over the eyes of a child drooling on a blue lollipop, and she was staring at me with unadulterated scorn.

"I said you can't ride this bus!" she snapped. "It's *indecent.*"

"Well I paid the fare, so—" I hefted the little backpack back over my shoulders, lurching as the bus began to move. The woman flinched back, glaring at me like I'd lunged at her. Her kid was just going to town on that lollipop.

"You have no right to be dressed that way in public," she continued, sticking out a leg to block my path. "If you can even call it being dressed. It's wrong. There are *children* here."

I looked down at the outfit in question, unable to stifle a disbelieving bark of laughter at being slapped with a scarlet letter on public transportation. This was becoming one hell of a Tuesday. "Yeah, I'm gonna sit down now."

I tried to step over her leg, and she raised her purse like some great moral barrier. Anger lit up the backs of my eyes in a swirl of sparking color. Fuchsia, fury, tangerine.

No one else on the bus said a word, no one made a move beyond just watching, and that, more than my own exposure, struck me with a horrible sense of translucence. Of wrongness, in space, time, and body.

Strangers were staring, and therefore I existed as the story they were telling about me in their heads. It made me sick. It made me protective.

What was I protecting?

A gaping void of nameless want. Some untended tale of a man and his spaceship; my tender, mechanical heart. The long-examined absence where the *she*-ness should be.

My hand shot up of its own volition, shoving the bag aside to further all the space between us. Our fingers touched, and that's when the vision came:

*It's snowing outside. The woman from the bus is walking into a restaurant that has real candles on the table, flames dancing underneath the chins of private diners like camp counselors holding flashlights. Her hair is a falling monument, her ankles twist grotesquely in her high heels, the tendons on her feet bulging. She is a vision of despair, her rage such a living squirming thing that no one interferes as she approaches a couple tucked away in a private booth. The man looks up, all conservative comfort and Hugo Boss. "Sharon?" he says with the look of someone who's been caught. "Daniel," the woman responds with the eerie calm of spousal fury. The twenty-something who sits across from Daniel doesn't even face the creature that's approached them, doesn't do anything but lock her eyes on the man who brought her here. Her delicate* SHE *stamp dances in the candlelight, and her expression is unreadable. Apathy? Anxiety? Pity? The woman, Sharon, she reaches for the younger woman's wine glass, drains it, lifts it, smashes it against her face.*

I yanked back, gasping, and was nearly thrown to the floor as the driver slammed on the brakes. The woman was really shouting now, something about how I had tried to attack her, but I couldn't hear her through the ringing in my ears.

"No fighting on my bus!" the driver bellowed, his booming baritone making the woman's son nearly drop his lollipop. "Off! You! Naked girl! Off the bus!"

"But I paid the fare," I said numbly. "And I'm not—"

"OFF."

The doors swung open and I stumbled onto the side of the road. We hadn't even made it to the mall's South Side stop. I looked up at the bus, stung by the injustice of the fact that I just paid three dollars to get yelled at in public by someone else's mother. I wanted to do something dramatic like fling a rock, or my bra. Really let loose. I don't know. Back then, when I was still a girl, trying to fit easily into a poorly made container, I didn't really know how to get angry. Like proper, lose-your-shit angry.

I'm not sure if I do now either. But that's another story.

As the bus drove away, I took one last stunned look at its window, catching sight of the back of the woman's head and beside it, the face of a small child. Her son, blue-mouthed and wide-eyed, staring at the monster banished to the side of the road. What would happen to him those months from now, when the glass came down?

I rubbed my face, taking a slow breath like my therapist taught me when I was six. It took a lot of work not to get sucked into other people's traumas, not to suffocate under the weight of all possible futures.

A car honked as it sped by, some guy leaning out of the passenger seat to holler at me.

"What are you looking at?!" I shouted back, but the car was already long gone. Probably for the best—me getting murdered by a frat boy on an ego trip was not something my mom needed to deal with right now.

Still, my own words echoed in my head, parching my throat:

*What are you looking at? What are you looking at? What are you looking at?*

The words pressed harder, squirming until the lightboard in my chest went dark. I walked toward the South Side stop, feeling the ugly desire to be shouted at one more time, to figure out what it was everyone was seeing when they looked at me.

*Meanwhile, in an intergalactic gambling den . . .*

The prince has never played a game of Falsehood in his life, but that doesn't stop him from putting down a substantial bet at the table. He props a leg up on the chair to his left, spreading his body carelessly while the chips magnetize and the holoboard resets for the round. Every act of posturing chips away at the amiable boy that was, refashioning him into a good-for-nothing rogue. It's the performance of a lifetime.

That's the point of the game, you see. It takes bluffing beyond the tiles and swerves straight into the territory of identity. In Falsehood, the players only speak in negatives, and it opens something like this:

*Your board has no lilies.*

*Your lilies hold no obsidian.*

*No red touches your fingers.*

It's a simple enough strategy, designed to reap easy points and set the stakes for the rest of the game. Once the players have something tangible to lose, the rounds progress to the personal:

*You've never trusted your lover with your money.*

*You know your mother isn't proud.*

*You haven't slept well in years.*

Falsehood is a game of conviction as much as it is a game of perception. Seasoned players face the tile boards with carefully cultivated personas, forcing opponents to dig for the truth while maintaining their own façade. When disputes are unable to be resolved, a glass sphere called an Arbiter sits in the middle, ready to display the truth and settle the score. More often than not, winning is dependent on what the accused are willing to tolerate, or sacrifice, for the sake of maintaining a good hand. Falsehood tables are most often frequented by cons and con artists, and the game is legal only in five locations across the galaxy, including its homeworld, Lvrna.

This magmic little blister of a planet is where the prince—rather, the rogue—is playing now, with entirely unearned confidence. This attitude, he tells himself, is how he will win.

The vanity scar he applied before hitting the casino feels tight and strange on his face, but his delicate features wouldn't very well sell his smuggler story, would they? The man across from him is built like an old dam, with arms bigger in circumference than the prince's whole torso; tonight he appears to be playing the role of the distinguished executive, powerful in his well-cut suit. His cufflinks are magmagold, and the drink in his hand costs more than fifty tickets to the buffet. They're about four rounds into the game, getting ready to shift into territory that makes the prince's pulse go seismic.

The slim, platinum communicator on his wrist buzzes once. The rogue's antennae twitch irritably; Bo is the only sentient being attached to that line, and he already told it that he didn't want to be bothered while he was out on Lvrna. It had put up such a stink about his choice to land here. *This is where you go first? A thousand planets, and you choose this? What do you have to prove so badly, Cornelius?*

"You don't have any Emperors," the rogue claims.

"Concede."

Points to the rogue. Another chip falls from the slot above them, magnetizes to his side of the table.

"Your hand holds no silver," the big man says.

"Dispute," the rogue replies calmly. "Challenge?"

"No."

Zero points to the big man. The rogue's eyes flash to the private holograms of his tiles. In the top right corner of his board, some Lvrnan death goddess is smiling with silver-inlaid teeth. He's not so bad at this, really. The big man might be ahead in points, but the rogue's getting better at bluffing, better at performing.

He swirls his drink. Most smugglers would have a sense of discretion, but he's decided to really play up this character. Arrogant, careless, a real small-time villain. Tonight, it would be in his interest to be just a bit underestimated. Bo warned him a dozen times not to get in over his head, but what does a chronically honest bot know about Falsehood?

The communicator feels heavy on the rogue's wrist. Maybe he should have responded to the messages at the start of this round, made sure that the ship wasn't in a total panic. But it wouldn't be true to his performance at the table. Besides, Bo's armed to the motherboard, and tucked far away from the scrap-hungry populace of Lvrna. The bot can take care of itself. And so can he.

*Dispute. Challenge. Falsehood.*

The servers pass by, moving so smoothly that the rogue can't tell if they're bionic or organic.

*Concede.*

He is surrounded on every side by liars. Some of the con artists cry out in delight when they are caught, pulling away disguises and buying drinks for the old friends they've uncovered.

*Dispute. Concede.*

Everyone's teeth look too sharp. It makes something in the rogue's belly roil low and hot. The music vibrates up through the foot he has placed on the ground, drowns out the sensation of Bo trying to get his attention with another message.

*Concede. Challenge. Truth.*

"You've never smuggled outside this star system."

The rogue is taken off guard by the sudden shift to the personal, but he plays it off as a bruised ego. To his relief, the accusation is technically true. "Concede," he says, sneering into his drink.

The big man looks pleased as his chips re-magnetize, and the rogue is planning his next move when the server approaches, offering refills. Their obsidian eyes are clear behind silver-dusted lashes, their fingers are long and slim upon the gilded tray, distinctly tattooed. The drink they are offering moves hypnotically in its decanter, lovely in a way that only truly dangerous things know how to be. Despite the fact that he's only had one glass, the big man shakes his head.

*"Shouldn't,"* he murmurs, trading the Lvrnan tongue for Krensh. *"Don't need to give the wife more to say about my drinking habits."*

As the server takes their leave, the rogue puts together the information he has just been given, however unintentional. Krensh is one of the major languages spoken on Shenshki, a major trade partner of the prince's homeworld, where servants and laborers have their fingers tattooed as a marker of status. His eyes flash to the big man's hands, which are concealed by dark gloves.

Convincing as his opponent's upper-class performance has been, the rogue suddenly recognizes the man's missteps. Falsehood is about more than physical presentation, after all; there are some tells that can't be shaken. Why would a man of authority use the language of the servant class? Why would he cover his hands? Why would someone so powerful care what his spouse thinks, or be married at all?

After draining his glass, the rogue makes his claim, sets his trap. "You've never swung a pickaxe."

"Dispute," the big man says. His brows raise a fraction. "Challenge?"

The rogue hesitates for only a moment. His opponent expects him to flinch, to back down at the lack of concession. The motions of Falsehood cramp in the rogue's mind, and he measures the risk: to challenge will lose him points, but when he sees the truth of the man's history as a common laborer, it will be easier to break down the rest of his lie. A worthy loss for a future gain. "Yes."

The big man rolls up a sleeve, swiping aside his private holoboard and resting a hand on the Arbiter. The liquid inside the glass orb swirls into a small tornado, then hardens to ice.

The rogue's stomach drops, and he looks down at the table where the man's memory, his proof, plays out.

In the memory, the big man holds a pickaxe, but he is not in the mines. There are others with him, but they are not laborers. A young man is knelt before him, gagged and weeping. The big man hefts the pickaxe before swinging it down not into rock, but into the bound man's skull.

The rogue is nearly sick on the table.

Things fall apart pretty quickly from there.

The big man cuts through him with systematic brutality, laying out claims which slaughter the rogue's points.

*You've never seen the inside of Lvrna's prisons.*

*You are followed by no warrants.*

*You are not at peace with your death.*

The rogue makes concession upon concession, not bothering to play smuggler any longer. His hands are shaking too hard to be persuasive, and Bo's buzzing only gets more insistent as the minutes pass. Much as he wants to shout at the bot to leave him alone, he wishes desperately that he could reply, fly far and fast from Lvrna, but the game isn't over. The big man's accusations are relentless, and the rogue, the prince, isn't delusional enough to think he has any chance in a battle of the personal. (Frankly, he would rather not watch anyone else die.) So he turns his attention to the tiles on the holoboard, playing a coward's game.

Between each blow to his ego, his pride, his personhood, the prince draws his own accusations against the big man's tiles, using the process of elimination to determine his board. Again and again he plays like it's the first round, never advancing to the cruelty Falsehood is made for. With no challenges made to the prince's own tiles, the points begin to even out, and the big man's expression gets darker, his accusations more pointed.

*You have no planned route out of here.*

*You've never smuggled before.*

*You don't yet know how it feels to beg for your life.*

"Your board no longer holds any deities," the rogue says, eyes on his holoboard.

"Concede," spits the big man, clenching his fists as the points drop once more. One final accusation is all it will take to end this game of Falsehood, but ultimately the payout will be nearly nothing. An easy win, a stolen victory. "Let's finish this off, you sour-stomached little punk. *You've never even played this game before.*"

The prince rubs his face, tugging at the vanity scar as he readies himself to concede and slink back to Bo. A waste of time and money, like the bot said. In way over his head, like everyone else said. Like they always say. Same game, different rules.

He stops. Stares into the face of the big man. Tries to think like Bo, like that brilliant popping lightboard.

"Well?" snaps the big man. "I said you've never played this game before. What's your answer? I haven't got all night."

A smile twitches at the corner of the prince's mouth. He dares. "Dispute."

"*Dispute?*" The big man laughs outright. "What kind of fool do you take me for, boy? Challenge!"

It's a bold move, and not one he's entirely sure will work, but there's no turning back from it. The prince rests his open palm on the Arbiter, holding his breath as it determines the temperature of his honesty. *It's true,* he thinks, *I've never played these tables before. I have no business on Lvrna. But he never specified the game. He never said the game was Falsehood.*

The Arbiter's liquid swirls, hardens to ice, and a flurry of scenes from his youth play out on the table. His many mothers, mourning his ridiculousness. His suitors, lusting after the approval of a half-formed idea and a royal stipend. His lovers, dismissing the truth in his tenderness, dismantling his protective shell. His Bo, redirecting their route again and again, insisting that the pilot has no idea what he's doing.

Surviving the world in small concessions, reassembling the self in pursuit of being taken seriously and loved nonetheless— Cornelius Flux has been playing this game for as long as he can remember. He has learned over the years to laugh off the losses, to pretend to be in on the joke. What has authenticity ever done for a soft heart?

His shame boils hot as any Arbiter's lie, but the scoreboard adjusts. The prince has won, his points amounting to just enough to cover the cost of the fuel that got Bo here. The big man looks ready to cut his throat, and probably would if the servers of Lvrna wouldn't have his head for shedding blood in the gambling den.

"Good game," the prince says as the chips de-magnetize. He picks them up, jangling them loosely in his fingers with a grim smile. "Play again sometime?"

He makes the walk back to Bo with haste, the eyes on his throat frantically seeking heat signatures that would indicate his being followed. His communicator is full of messages from the bot, messages that grow more vehement with each timestamp.

The colors of the most recent ones hurt his upper set of eyes. A critical fuchsia, an unhappy xanthic yellow. They tug something in him that he can't explain. He calls the ship, cringing against the beeping and crackling that greets him over audio.

"I'm fine, Bo," he says. His tongue tingles with the aftertaste of his drink. His hands tremble with every flush of adrenaline. "The game ran long. Nothing happened, the game just ran long."

The ship doesn't believe him, and it shouldn't, but to be caught in another lie is to be made small. The rogue bites down on his version of the story, ignores the ache in his jaw. "I said *nothing happened*. I don't know why you have to be like that. It was a fun night—I won, even. So just be happy for me, would you? Let it go."

*iii.*

Given the way the day started, the rain wasn't much of a surprise. I didn't have it in me to be upset about the weather—if anything, I nearly appreciated the splash of pathetic fallacy. It's sort of nice when the world sees you struggling and goes *wait, mood piece!* rather than surrounding you with images of everyone else who's more well-adjusted than you are.

It's not like I quit a job a week back then, when I was still a girl. I just fell into this pattern where I'd find tolerable situations and dress them up as enjoyable, claim them as possible turning points. For the first four months or so I'd take any shift, be anyone's confidante, fall in love with any place that looked like it needed it. Anywhere that let me take my shoes off became a home, a touchstone of identity that I clung to with a surreal, inexplicable determination. Then one day I'd have this out-of-body experience and get smacked with the realization that I didn't even like this. I wasn't even happy. Why was I working so hard to make everyone believe I was happy?

I never managed to stay long after that. The visions got to be too much. I couldn't show up on time. I'd miss phone call after phone call. But it wouldn't feel bad, really.

Admitting this doesn't do much for my resume, but when the time came, I never felt bad about leaving. It was like a snake shedding skin, itching and writhing until the burden sloughed off for some weird kid to find and put in a shoebox. For as long as I could avoid hitting reset on the whole game, it felt like I could breathe in the void that was left between identities. Disappearing gave me a thick endorphin rush, like I was being called and comforted by some sort of *urge* to step back from all discomfort without examining its source.

My body, on the other hand, was always slow on the uptake, nagging me with this bone-deep dread that left me tonguing my fillings, searching for a taste of what kept going wrong. It was tiring, carrying some blissed-out inner world in such a chary body—mostly I passed the time reading pulpy sci-fi trade paperbacks the local library got in their donation bin.

I shifted my backpack in my lap, wishing I'd brought a book even though I couldn't read it in the rain. And my phone was at like 8%, because of course it was, so I had it on airplane mode. The wistfulness of the whole experience was starting to evaporate pretty quickly as the temperature dropped. I rubbed the gooseflesh on my arms, teeth chattering as I began to reevaluate my notions of what a day in late April was supposed to feel like.

Then the car pulled up, right to the curb. My SHE stamp was pretty much a lost cause at this point, but that didn't stop the *Now That's What I Call Time To Get Murdered!* soundtrack that started playing in my head. My mom had a thing for true crime shows, and I had this chronic fear of really ruining one of the high holidays by being found in a quarry somewhere. Probably unrelated.

The car window rolled down and a raspy tenor voice came out: "Hey, do you need a ride?"

"I'm waiting for the bus," I said, glancing up at him for a brief moment, trying to look uninterested. There was something familiar about him, the lilt in his voice or the way one eye squinted a little more than the other. *(Did you know that most kidnappings are carried out by friends or family?)*

"It's raining," the guy continued, "and you look kind of . . . cold? Plus you weren't in the food court today, so..."

"Oh, shit—Froyo Kid?"

Froyo Kid was my private name for the guy who worked at, you guessed it, the frozen yogurt place that stood sentinel beside the ghost town that had once been a Sears and would eventually become a Spirit Halloween.

It was also a name I had not called him in person, *because why would anyone do that*. I opened my mouth to apologize, but he looked amused. "My degrading little branded hat is off, so you can probably get away with just calling me Theseus."

*Theseus?* How did I not know that was his name before? I didn't think that was what the name tag said. The car door unlocked with a loud *thnk*.

"Seriously," he said, squinting at the darkening rain clouds, "can I offer you a ride?"

I took in the risk factor. A seemingly inoffensive guy who usually gives me frozen yogurt in the food court, driving a fantastically shitty old 2001 Buick LeSabre with a big scratch down the side, half-covered by a bumper sticker in the shape of a bandaid. The froyo came out of a machine, so it didn't require as much muscle strength as scooping ice cream, so I could probably take him in a fight. Plus he agreed the hat was super degrading.

"Yeah, actually," I said. "I'd appreciate it."

Froyo Kid—sorry, *Theseus*—cleared away the mandatory pile of garbage on the passenger seat, and I shuffled in, immediately grateful for the car heater and the startling amount of legroom. I envied the old takeout bag on the floor, the odd leaf caught in the rug, the change stuck to the cupholders; I'd wanted to buy a car since I'd moved back home, but never seemed to let myself put the money down for it.

Theseus pulled out a relic of a GPS, handing it to me. "Would you put your address in?"

"I can just give you directions," I said, buckling in the seatbelt. It dug into my skin in a way that felt unfamiliar; most of my car rides weren't performed topless.

"Alright so I promise this isn't anything weird," he began, instantly making me think it was something weird, "but I will definitely get us lost if it's not in the GPS."

". . . what?" I laughed.

"I'm serious," he said, looking at me solemnly. There was something on his left cheek, some sort of smudge, but I couldn't make it out from the passenger seat. "I can only obey the TomTom. And before you ask, using the map on my phone is worse. It suggests a faster route, I panic and smash some buttons, then it takes twice as long. Swear on the flavor of the day, I am not fucking with you. It's a curse."

"A curse?"

"A curse. We'll end up in a whole other dimension."

Behind my eyes, a dozen screens played, blinking cinematic as the security room of a museum I couldn't remember the name of. I saw swaths of fabric made starlight, swirling through a ballroom. I saw something that could have been a dragon, or a great big fish. I saw purple hands, feathered hands, clawed hands, mechanical hands. A child that could not sit still. The ghosts of a thousand misplaced pens. A body that was a ship, putting itself together piece by piece, sheltering the small ache inside. The ache itself, raging against its lonely shelter.

I put my address into the GPS, listening to the friction of the wipers against the glass.

Theseus kept his music at a reasonable volume, not so loud that I felt suffocated, but not quiet enough to demand conversation. I mean, it would have been awkward if we just sat there in silence, but what I mean is that it felt good to have a second to breathe. To not feel like the space was gawking at me, wanting something. Empty space could be such a fucking carnivore.

The first words that found their way to my mouth were, predictably, inane and possibly a little insulting: "So ... Theseus, huh?"

He laughed, tugging down the beanie he was wearing in place of the usual Froyo Dipz hat. "Theodore's on the license. But I go by Theseus. When I was living in the city there were like ... two other Theodores or Théophiles or whatever in my friend group, so parties were pretty confusing."

"Two Theodores?" I asked. Even for the city, it didn't seem like a super common name. Usually classrooms in these dead-eyed suburban towns stuck to the classic lineup: three Matts, four Mikes, Sean, Shaun, and Shawn.

"It's kind of a trans guy thing to name ourselves like Victorian kittens. Don't ask me why. You wouldn't believe the number of Felixes and Olivers I've met." He shook his head with a haunted look that made me laugh. There was an expressiveness to Theseus that made him easy to look at, to listen to. I wondered how he pulled it off; I had never really figured out how to wear my own face, a tangle of muscle and hesitation.

"So you decided to switch things up to the totally low-key *Theseus*?"

He grinned a little, shrugging as he merged onto a brief stretch of highway. "It was like a metaphor, I guess? Less Theseus the hero and more the whole concept of the ship." A spark popped deep in my chest, a flickering light I didn't have the words for. I nodded quickly to show that I understood, but I didn't have the verbal language to describe just how *much*. "I was changing a lot back then, thinking about what I was adding and subtracting to my whole notion of self. Who I'd end up as, or what. Maybe it sounds a little goofy, but it made sense for me. And I liked it better than my mom's suggestion."

"Which was?"

"Jeffrey."

"Spell it with a G-e-o and it's almost a Victorian cat name," I offered, and he laughed, bright and charming. It rang against the soothing soundscape: the rain tapping against glass, the glass humming against the rattling of the car, the car growling against the cool of the outdoors. In the background, increasingly bizarre experimental music.

"Thanks again for picking me up," I said, tugging absently at my seatbelt. "Today's been a weird one."

"You want to talk about it?" Theseus asked.

I wasn't sure. I was still a little rattled from watching that lady on the bus smash a glass in her husband's mistress' face some time this coming winter, but that wasn't exactly a first car ride conversation. And I still didn't know where it was in my body that I could find the words to explain how perfectly monstrous I felt tossing my shirt at my boss by the fountain. I glanced at the clock—4:22pm. The call to regional management had long passed.

"I quit my job," I ended up saying, finding comfort in minimization. "And then I got kicked off the bus for being indecent."

"What were you doing?" Theseus asked, and all at once I remembered to be furious.

"Nothing!" I said, rubbing my face, leaving the SHE stamp all over my palm like a mutinous black spot. I pressed my hands into my jeans, smearing it away. "I just wasn't wearing a shirt."

"And they kicked you off? That's total bullshit."

"Right?!" An immeasurable sense of relief slammed into my chest at the confirmation of my own sanity. "Such bullshit, total bullshit. And I'd still have a shirt if I hadn't quit, but I had to quit, so I turned it in—"

"Wait, like, right off your back?" Theseus looked at me with something that might have been respect. Once more I caught a glimpse of the mark on his cheek, where his SHE stamp would have been if he were a woman. But men didn't wear stamps—they were just allowed to Be.

"Yeah," I said, trying not to lean over too obviously and snoop on his face, wondering if it counted as snooping if it was somewhere that everyone could see. "I don't just walk around tits out at the mall for the fun of it. I was . . . making a statement or something? And I really didn't want to go back to return it later."

"Good for you," Theseus said with a nod, turning right on the GPS's command, into the part of town where the trees leaned across the road to brush branches. "It's got to feel pretty good, acting on one of the good old quitting fantasies."

"I think so," I said, and it wasn't completely a lie.

The rest of the ride filled itself with more of those not-completely-lies:

*You look happy enough at Froyo Dipz, even with the awful hat.*

*Concede. You're pretty prepared to just go toward whatever comes next, huh?*

*Dispute. Challenge?*

We skimmed the fractured surface of stories that you can't spring on near-strangers without looking unstable, made sideways glances at the underbellies of things that usually get saved for sleepaway camp or self-indulgent journaling. Back then, connecting with people beyond the visions was a constant struggle. I hadn't yet learned how to be something other than a receptacle for other people's needs. It made me a brief friend. A worse partner.

That car ride had chemistry. Not the intense, sexual Hollywood chemistry, shaped with obvious looks and embarrassing shots of people's necks and forearms, but chemistry as in a *reaction*, as in some core elements crashing together and sparking, grasping at each other in search of becoming something more. I didn't really like his music, but I liked the way he didn't make that weird *isn't-it-cool-how-much-we're-vibing* face or demand I laugh at his jokes. I liked that he sometimes applied his staff discount to my froyo in exchange for samples of salt scrub.

Connecting with people had always felt a little like losing opacity, like offering up parts of me that even I couldn't see. The closest I ever got was being curious.

When we pulled up to my house and he turned to say goodbye, I noticed three things about his face: a pale hazel ring in his left iris, a small hole where a lip ring must have been once—

*a HE stamp, placed delicately on his left cheek.*

When he smiled, the stamp nudged up toward his eye, reaching for the ring of light around his pupil.

And I was curious.

*Meanwhile, where body heat refuses to rise . . .*

The prince is caught beneath a body that runs several degrees cooler than his own, but is lovely enough in texture that he thought he wouldn't mind. When their seven slim fingers scraped over his soft belly, back on the lunar base, he imagined he might even enjoy it. That was the point of this trip, wasn't it? To travel places his mothers would disapprove of, to do the things no one thought him capable of, to take lovers at his leisure and build himself a reputation without the weight of public veneer. He left to have a good time.

*I like a lot of things*, the prince thinks to himself, remembering to breathe. *What does it even mean to like something, anyway?*

The lights are low in the back room of the B.O.D.Y. unit as the prince reminds himself to be in the moment, reminds himself to be a rogue, to enjoy this new experience. Music vibrates against skin stretched tight over spine as he tries to forget the shame the Falsehood table left in his bones. He moans into a sharpened kiss, his body overwrought and sensitive against the frosty heat of another.

The name of his partner fits poorly in the shape of his mouth, so he seeks a better use for his tongue. Their many sliding, squirming limbs wrap around him like a vice, holding him still as they sink into him. It is too deep, too much, and not enough; the rogue shivers, shudders with something implacable and uncanny. The touch of nails is too light on the backs of his thighs. His own sweat feels obscene.

His partner growls something in a language he doesn't understand, slackens their grip on him just so. The rogue whimpers as his antennae twitch, searching for the lost source of that suffocating compression. Their limbs suddenly tighten back around him, prompting a startled cry. He does not understand why he is shaking. He has done this so many times before. The alien has long been the erotic; mutual understanding has always been attained most easily in the dark. He tries to steady his fearful heart, soothe himself with familiarity. Back home, in his own bed, tied up by the visiting daughter of an ambassador—

*Home?*

      *You're so*                     *far*     *from home.*

          *(You've never even played this game before.)*

    *You are*

         *such a soft*            *and helpless*

                              *thing.*

Adrenaline spikes through languid dopamine, makes the rogue a prince again, so very far away. His voice struggles through the fog of his constructed want, and the first breath of his *no* has barely been taken when all the lights in the ship slam on. Alarms blare, and Bo's bulbs pop urgently. (Furiously.)

"I-I'm sorry—" the rogue begins, wincing as his partner

pulls from him too suddenly, too fast. He is left slick and empty, pushing his hair back from his face as he struggles to get to the switchboard in a dignified manner. "My unit was running some background diagnostics, it must have—it must have found something."

Bo's lights circle and brighten, performing myriad demands in bursts of orange and jade. The rogue's gut drops in understanding, but he isn't about to undermine his ship in front of a stranger. It is Bo's interior, after all. He looks back to his partner, thankful they can't understand a word of the B.O.D.Y.'s light language, and sees their many limbs are already reconstructing into a more bipedal shape. As their flesh remodels itself into the image of the lunar base's uniform, he finds himself vaguely envious of their malleability, their graceful transparence.

"I'm sorry," he says again, reaching for his discarded clothing and clutching it in his lap. He feels exposed without the body of another covering his. He is cold down to his bones. "My ship needs manual assistance with a reboot and it's—it's going to take a while. You should probably go."

They shrug, a non-committal rippling motion that seems to lack malice. Unfairly, this pangs at the rogue; it's not like he was looking to spurn a lover, but he wishes they'd protest at least a little. Wasn't it going well? Weren't they both having a good time?

A final kiss dances over the back of the prince's neck, making his throat eyes squeeze shut against the cold, and then the stranger slips out of the door. It closes heavily behind them, and all of the alarms stop at once as the lights dim back down to something soothing. Even Bo's talking bulbs go quiet, waiting for the prince to speak first. It's unlike the ship, not to dive in for the first word. Or the last.

The rogue grits his teeth and gets up, excusing himself to the washroom. A thin mist of decontaminant steams over his skin, and he stays there until he is warm again. He pats dry with a towel, angry without the words to say why.

*(You have no planned route out of here.)*

He pulls on a spidersilk robe, a small homeworld indulgence he couldn't bring himself to part with, and tries to remoor his mind to the persona he aspires to. As he steps back out into the main room, he sees that Bo has pulled up instructions for a Float. This is one of the unit's best ways of resetting, when most of the main functions go dormant for a few hours, leaving the ship to bob gently in the vacuum of space, recalibrating between shifting atmospheres. It's also one of the rogue's favorite ways they spend time together, a relic of the early days of their relationship.

The B.O.D.Y. unit cannot handle the silence any longer. It has always gotten nervous when its companion pulls away like this. Beside the prince, its talking bulbs swirl pale and soothing jade.

The rogue clenches his fists. "I'm fine, Bo."

The colored lights tessellate all along the ship, growing only fractionally brighter.

"Yes, I'm sure."

The lights shrink in on themselves; a hum of white, patterning doubtfully across the low ceiling. The ship's concern flutters like falling ash blossoms—

"I said it's fine!" the prince snaps. Something inside him

expands its ugliness, filling the space where he best holds his shame. "You didn't need to interfere, you know. I didn't need your help."

Bo levels him with an irritable splash of orange before it adjusts its processing; the prince has never been the de-escalating type. If the ship loses its temper, there's no saving him from himself. It tries to shift back to the pale jade of before, but the color is muddied, sour. The prince cannot accept the ship's concern, but is quick to latch onto its impatience.

He steps into his quarters and closes the door without another word. The conversation is far from finished, but Bo loves him enough to maintain the illusion of privacy and keep it shut.

*iv.*

Cult's kind of a loaded word.

When I talk about being raised in a cult, I don't mean it in the late-night special context. More along the lines of the Greco-Roman mysteries—full of secrets too well-guarded to survive history and make it into aesthetically tight but ultimately shallow film adaptations. Maybe this doesn't make sense.

What I'm getting at is that back then, when I was still a girl, my family raised me in the cult of the divine, empowered feminine. They aligned womanhood with strength and survival, fought back against the greater prevailing tumor known as the cult of domesticity. They gave me books on badass women throughout history. They called a vagina a vagina instead of a foo-foo or a cookie or whatever other name anxious parents tell their kids so they don't shame the family in the middle of an IHOP.

In my home, being a woman wasn't about being a man's equal—it was about having something *more*. A sacred piece of core programming, beloved and often misunderstood. As far back as my great-great-great-grandmother, who legend had it made a name for herself as a mystic in what my grandmother nebulously called *the old country*, every first child had been born a daughter. Our endurance in a man's world was a point of pride, and at every family function, all of the living first daughters would stand together for a photo taken by one of the grumbling second sons. Strong women, strong women—in the home, the synagogue, the street. I stood at the end of the line, hands in my pockets, smiling nervously as everyone claimed my visions as points toward my womanhood. They looked at each other, the mysteries flowing between them like cosmic feminine ley lines, and I felt nothing.

Before my grandmother died, she took my face in her knotted hands. She hushed me as I shuddered, watching my family weeping over her casket in the months to come. "You have the gift, daughter of daughters," she said, and I didn't know if it was more her pride or my shame that made me so determined to be a girl.

In a world that wielded womanhood as a silencing tool, I had been born into the mysteries, graced with the knowledge of inherited power. Cult's kind of a loaded word, but what I'm trying to say is that even though I knew that I didn't belong, leaving didn't feel like an option.

Sorry. That got heavier than I expected. It's still hard sometimes, rewiring new perspective to old circuitry.

Anyway, I had Theseus drop me off a little bit down the street in case he decided last minute to be an axe-murderer. There was always the risk of my neighbors seeing me running down the street topless, but I didn't really have it in me to be worried about what the gossip might be at a church that I didn't even attend. Before I left, he gave me his number. "In case you miss the froyo," he said.

I was thinking about how bad the froyo was and how not-half-bad Theseus was as I snuck in over the flower pots and through the back door, trying not to get my mom's attention. My luck ran out when I slammed my ankle into one of the boxes that had been stacked haphazardly in the sunroom, still not yet unpacked even after moving in seven years ago. We had never been good at getting rid of things, or settling in.

I unleashed a stream of curses, hobbling into the kitchen to find my mother standing with her arms crossed, a thumb tucked in her novel as a placeholder.

Despite my premonitions, it sometimes scared the shit out of me to see my body's possible futures in the woman who made me. So much of us was the same: the thick, dark head of hair, the wide hips and too-big feet, the identical ridge on the nose, pronounced over a sharp cupid's bow.

"Is that my half-nude daughter putting hexes on my home?" she asked, cocking an eyebrow.

"No," I muttered, tossing my bag on the counter. "Just a criminal come to save you from yourself by kicking down the fire hazard you've put on display."

She laughed, turning on the kettle for tea. "Are you still a criminal if I pay you to do the right thing and burn it altogether?"

This was an old ritual we had. I'd come home from school upset, she'd put on tea and pull out the ginger snaps. Even as an adult, I couldn't hide anything from her.

"Well if there are any careers opening up in the arson field, I am looking for work."

Silence passed between us, that beat of discomfort where

I watched my mother go from her own person to a parent, searching for the thing to say that wouldn't become a lasting personal trauma. Her fingers grasped for nothing and she pushed back her flyaways, fingers nudging her SHE stamp as she chose her words.

"You got fired . . . ?" she asked cautiously, taking down two mismatched mugs from our battered old hutch.

"I quit, actually." I sat down on a stool, resting my head on the kitchen counter and waiting for my brain to stop over-heating. "But they probably would have fired me eventually. I wasn't really . . ." Right for the job? Meeting my sales quota? *She* enough? "It wasn't working out."

"Their loss," she said matter-of-factly, giving my shoulder a squeeze that prompted a vision of her pulling chicken out of the oven later tonight. To my dismay, she had some alien conspiracy theory show on the television in the background.

"Their loss," I echoed, squashing my nose against the ceramic tiles. Maybe it was the kid in me, but those *you're-my-baby-and-I-love-you* reassurances were more comforting than they had any right to be. Unlike pretty much every other woman in our family, my mom hadn't planned on having children. I was a surprise in her second year of art school, and she decided to take the least predictable route and just roll with it. Lucky for me, she turned out to be a pretty good parent.

Now I just had to figure out how to be lucky for her right back. As far as moms go, she gave me a lot of room to not suck: no demands to procreate or pay rent, no shaming me over my shitty mall job, no throwing a fit when my semester off turned into two years off. Hell, she put me in therapy when I was four years old, "just to give you a head start on wherever I'm going wrong." She liked it when my SHE stamp was put on messy, thought I was really establishing myself as my own woman. A woman of the future.

I closed my eyes, listening to the electricity rush through the kettle, readying itself to magician water into gas into noise.

She sat down beside me, opening up the ginger snaps. "Can I ask about it?"

"Can I decline to answer?"

"If it'll make you feel better." She got up to make the tea, poking one of my freckles on her way by. I wrinkled my nose. The freckles had been a gift from my father in lieu of child support, and she'd never been able to keep her hands off of them.

I stuffed a ginger snap in my mouth, trying to figure out why doing the right thing had put me in such emotional limbo.

"I think I hated it there," I said, swallowing. "And I didn't really know it until I saw myself leaving."

I felt her attention perk up, her flutter of pride fill the space. The aroma of the steeping Darjeeling sunk into my skin, clinging to my lungs like a nervous child.

"Well, the visions don't lie, do they?"

"Nope." It was sometimes a relief, having the visions there to absolve me of the responsibility that came with choice. As much as they interrupted my day-to-day life, I always felt a little naked when I would touch someone and be met with visual silence.

"Did you see your future as a nudist?" she asked conspiratorially, and I laughed in spite of myself. It had gotten harder to take my problems so seriously in the past couple of years, took less time to lean into the humor of a foul situation. There wasn't so much fucking art to make out of every inconvenience.

So we drank tea and ate ginger snaps while I told her the story of my grand exodus, told her how much better lotion there was out there. To my personal agony, she admitted that she hated the smell of the stuff I'd been getting her but didn't want to scorn a gift from her kid. The rain came down harder. We finished the box of cookies. When my mom started complaining that she had no idea what to do for dinner, I let her know she'd be baking a chicken, and that those conspiracy shows were just playing reruns tonight so she might as well pick a movie.

"I don't know how I got anything done before you," she said, digging through the freezer to find the chicken she apparently had. "Worth the few years without sleep. And that time you vomited on my laptop."

"Mom," I groaned.

"Just all over it. Everywhere."

"I was six!"

"First week at the new, salaried job. My first and only corporate gig. They gave me a laptop, which they didn't give to everyone back then, and you just—"

"Vomited, yeah," I repeated, flicking tea in her direction. "Absolutely everywhere. Got under every key. I've heard this one a million times."

She laughed, blowing her hair out of her face and looking so quintessentially *my mother* that it made my chest hurt. "I did quit about three months after that," she mused. "So maybe you had it right. The boss was a real misogynist prick. Don't know if I ever told you that."

"You didn't." I sat up, waiting for the story. But she said nothing, placing the chicken in a bowl of warm water to defrost. When she turned, leaning against the counter, her SHE stamp seemed to look back at me, its bold terracotta lettering sat confidently on her high cheekbone. It looked like it belonged there, like she had been born with all of the right parts already in place, like all the goddess imagery in the world manifested into something tangible and kissed her.

The lingering navy on my cheek felt like a crushed insect, smeared by the heel of someone else's shoe.

"Mom—" I started to say.

"Mom, I have something to tell you," I failed to say.

"Mom, I have something I need to tell you," I said in some unreachable, impossible plane. "I don't know what's wrong with me. I don't know how to be your daughter. I don't know how to be anyone's daughter. I don't think I even know what womanhood is, and that's why I failed at my job, because I couldn't do it right, and they needed me to do it, to perform for them. Does that make sense? Have you ever felt this way? Is this just what it's supposed to be like?"

I was frozen in the great stillness of potential, a thousand unsaid words turning to screws in my mouth, tumbling and scraping up my tongue as I sought the proper timeline. All my possible futures lived and died in that endless breath of a moment, spectacular from inception through supernova. I ground my feet into reality, yearning and yearning—

"Mom—" I started to say.

"Oh!" she said faster than I could find my courage. "If you got fired—"

"Quit."

"If you quit your job, that means you're free this Saturday." She tapped at the refrigerator calendar, looking at me hopefully.

"What's happening Saturday?" I got up, grabbing one of the blankets on the couch and wrapping it around myself. I was shaken by the sense that I had just missed something very important, and the pressure on my shoulders was soothing. It made me feel like my feet were on the ground. It made me feel like Stellaluna.

"It's Aunt Lisa's birthday," she said, quickly trying to get the rest of her words out before I could start arguing. "And trust me, I know how you feel about those barbecues. But I *am* your mother and I don't want to go alone because however much you don't like them, they like *me* even less."

"Then why are you going?" I groaned. "Phil's going to be there."

"Uncle Phil's tough, I know."

"Phil *sucks*."

"Phil sucks," she conceded. "But Lisa is my sister, even if we harbor very different notions about what qualifies as success and happiness and basic decency. We stay for an hour and a half and then one of us fakes an emergency. Please?"

I wanted to argue, but I honestly didn't have a good enough excuse. Besides, when she started making the kicked puppy face on Saturday, I'd end up going anyway. Easier to get the arguing out of the way now. "Fine. Ninety minutes."

"That's my girl," she said, giving me a squeeze through my

blanket cape. I tried to wiggle an arm free, to find some skin to meet her hands, to seek the futures I feared most. But by then she'd pulled away, and I had lost my nerve to look.

*Meanwhile, when all the lights are quiet . . .*

The prince sleeps. He is a gentle sight, tucked against the round window at the back of the ship. Though his top set of eyes are closed, the eyes on his throat are open, gazing tenderly at a distant stellar nursery. Yearning for the heat that pierces through the unyielding cold of the void. At this corner of the cosmos, everything is quiet.

Bo finds this to be relieving. Its pilot has not slept well since they first left the homeworld those weeks ago—and slept even worse since leaving Lvrna. He is always fluctuating, tumultuous. Pacing, anxious, and then tossing and turning once his sleep cycles begin. There is urgency and there is listlessness, each competing to trouble him, the one Bo loves most in all the universe.

Hours do not mean much to a B.O.D.Y. unit. It has been alive from the start, in one way or another. It will be alive all the way to the end. It is not so for an organic.

Before Bo constructed itself a body, it was a ball of ylem, an impassioned cluster of neurons and potential. It lived in the peace of infinite possibility, secure in the knowledge that whatever it was now, it could become something new in the future.

But right now, it is a ship. Now, it is a home.

Often, these days, Bo is not so sure if it is doing a very good job being a home. It runs the air through its filters, clears out the water, controls the volume, warms the food, travels anywhere from a warp to a crawl—but does it nurture? Does it tend?

The prince sleeps, and the ship worries.

Today, the prince has forgotten to bring a blanket to the window. Beside him, a cup of floral tea sits untouched, long since gone cold. The edge of a screw digs into his bare arm, a temporary white imprint in the smooth lavender. All of his functions are running as they should, his blood velvet, his organs rich and healthy. But the sorrow. What does a B.O.D.Y. do for sorrow?

The ship wishes, as always, that it could open up the prince's motherboard and understand what is misfiring. It longs for the ability to program a Float for his racing thoughts, reset him to something that would hurt them both a little less.

Instead, it opens its own walls with a quiet hiss, extending the small mechanical grasps the prince calls its hands. It pats around his room until it finds something suitably warm, then passes the quilt from grasp to grasp until it reaches the observation hub and the sleeping creature inside. The body of the ship is kept at an optimal temperature—Bo has checked many times—but sometimes organics need material comforts.

The bot understands, in its way. The last time its interior paneling needed to be replaced, everything was discombobulated, imbalanced. When the new sheets of shimmering opal were finally put in, it just felt more *complete*. It cannot help the rush of tender binary that hums through its system when it remembers that Cornelius was the one to suggest the color.

Cornelius. That is the name his mothers gave him. Bo knows this, and is grateful that it does not have a mouth to speak it, instead translating it into flashes of color. The boy has always cringed back from his name. His titles. His personhood.

Bo doesn't know why the homeworld's organics are so fixated on personhood, why so many rules are constructed around it, so many limits and qualifications imposed. When B.O.D.Y. units fail to respect their own internal workings and the limitations of their ylem, they are likely to misfunction, to fall right out of the sky along with those they carry. A machine must know its specs, not the nature of its being.

But what are the real consequences of an organic's skewed perception of personhood? Why are they so afraid of not being when they are so clearly *there*?

The scaled lids of the prince's lower eyes blink slowly. Bo opens and closes its camera.

An interruption—an incoming signal reaches the B.O.D.Y., and promptly becomes *signals*, plural. Its transmitter stutters out messages that must have been held in the backlog while Bo was reserving its power for their next long-distance journey. Bo reprioritizes its functions, pausing the water heater repair in favor of interpreting the binary into messages the prince will be able to understand.

It reads them, of course. Bo is the prince's friend, but it is also a ship, and it cannot help its functions. Bit by bit, it unravels the distant code into the language of the prince's homeworld.

There are messages from his mothers, his suitors, those who would call themselves friends. Politicians and journalists, media media media. Bo reads through invitations and flirtations, everything from a curt single-line demand to a winding letter carved out in raw and pulsing grief.

In the translation functions, the ship witnesses an infinity of hands grabbing at its Cornelius. Not with tender mechanical grasps, but with hunger, with need. They need him to be everything; they need him to be exactly what they want him to be.

And the ship is afraid.

Bo's heat sensors lock on the small warmth curled up in the observation deck, the many delicate engines pulsing within him. The ship has been told that sorrow is felt in the heart, but the prince's vitals appear to be in sound condition.

And yet the tea. And yet the forgetfulness. And yet the stories he will not tell after adventures that do not make him happy.

The messages snake through Bo's transmitter, looping patiently. It is expected that Bo would place them somewhere the prince can see, that it would offer up a small hum to signal their presence. Strong communication is a hallmark of a B.O.D.Y. unit's primary functions, honesty is true to its coding; of course, this would be more apparent if the prince had the capacity to *listen* for once.

Perhaps it is a fault of biology. Organics are not the same as bionics; to look is not to read is not to comprehend. No reason to feel so smug about all those eyes. The words must first be passed over before they can pass through.

There is a wound in Cornelius that Bo cannot see. There is something in his heart that it cannot find and repair, not in the way it wants to, and it fears what these messages will do if they take root. A bit of bad code can corrupt everything, and the ship does not want its friend to break.

And so it opens up its circuitry, rerouting each cruel and kind word to somewhere private. If the prince really wants them, he can look. If he goes looking, Bo won't stop him.

The prince keeps secrets all the time—perhaps it would be better if the B.O.D.Y. did the same. Maybe this small lie could be what helps him preserve his personhood, which matters so much to him.

The B.O.D.Y. scans for any incoming threats, corrects its course and recalibrates the levels of ylem that power its systems. It flutters through the great tapestry of space, carefully navigating through the debris that would knock it into nothing. The flight is so smooth that Cornelius does not wake for many hours, and the ship is proud.

It is not so hard, the B.O.D.Y. thinks, to do the right thing.

*v.*

When we got to Aunt Lisa's, it took less than half an hour before I started fantasizing about pressing people's faces into the grill. This wasn't something I was particularly proud of. Back then (and even now, if I'm being honest), it disturbed the hell out of me when my anger got that visceral. It's like when your middle school counselor tells you that you can be as depressed as you want, seriously, join the club kid, as long as you don't have *A Plan*.

Imagining the horrified screams of the neighbors felt like I was drifting gradually closer to Plan territory, and that required the kind of therapy I definitely did not have the insurance for.

I scooped more potato salad onto my styrofoam plate, thinking about how easy it is to just buy something recyclable while I tried to tune out the jokes that the men around me were making. They were quoting some recently-disgraced comedian that hated women, laughing about how much they also hated women while my Aunt Lisa tutted at them for hating women and insisted to my mother that they didn't *really* hate women and she doesn't see why people don't get that it's just a joke and people are so sensitive these days and oh, also, why shouldn't she be allowed to have a *straight* pride parade if all of these gays get to storm around the city in their underwear?

"You hear about those *vegans?*" Uncle Phil said to one of his buddies, way too loudly. They gathered around him like vultures to a carcass, looking for something good to tear off for themselves. "This guy I work with, apparently his son's a *vegan* now. Can you think of anything more fucking embarrassing? The other night, he told the kid he'd bought this extra special *vegan* meat, just for him. So the kid bites into it, then spits it all over when he realizes it's plain old pork. Funny, it looked delicious when he thought it was made of tofu!"

The laughter made me nauseous. I wondered how I could reconcile my passion for reproductive justice with my belief that some people really just shouldn't be allowed to reproduce.

"A fucking vegan, can you imagine?!"

Look, I wasn't exactly a friend to all vegans myself, but at least I could have a conversation with them about the nuances of ethical consumerism. There was no way to reason with people who got off on eating meat in some bizarre act of hyper-masculine performance art.

I looked at my mother, wanting to ask about bailing early, but she was trapped with Aunt Lisa in a conversation about what actually qualifies as a human right. Aunt Lisa never made any sense to me. Like I said earlier, the women in my family prided themselves in their strength. More spice than sugar. Women's retreats, read-alongs of *The Red Tent*. Power in solidarity.

But the message never landed with Aunt Lisa, who married a lump of a misogynist and turned into everything the matriarchal line had ever spoken against. I guess there's a rebel in every family.

Aunt Lisa's way of life terrified me, backed me into a

corner. Was shying away from *the divine feminine* of my line an act of violence against my own? A projection of internalized misogyny?

I didn't want to hate women. I just didn't know how to *be* one.

"Aw, what's that face, *She?*" Phil said, apparently deciding he needed a new target. "You a vegan too, now?" His vulture friends hopped around, carnage hanging from their mouths. I didn't know what was so funny.

"Well I'm eating chicken right now," I said dryly, "so obviously not."

*"Obviously not,"* he repeated in a squeaky voice that was supposed to be me. I thought about my hands fisted in his hair, slamming down his face right where his *HE* stamp would be if he had to wear one, but instead it would say *Run Away* or *It's Easy to Be Cruel, Just Watch* or *Some People Are Beyond Helping And You Need To Accept That Eventually.*

He started to say something else, but I was already walking away, trying to get the grotesque image out of my head. Trying not to take so much pleasure in it. My mother must have seen the look on my face, because she tried to wave me over. *Bathroom*, I mouthed, and took the out I had made for myself.

I locked the door behind me, sucking in a breath through my teeth. Being with these people always made me feel this way. My mom always said she didn't like it either, but she still managed to begrudgingly interact with everyone. Meanwhile, all I could do was watch in dull horror, trying to imagine what it was like to live that way, and too afraid to touch anyone and find out.

My skin felt too tight, all wrong. I stared in the bathroom

mirror, trying to understand this version of myself that was trapped in flesh. It was easier to be a metaphor of a body. A piece of faulty architecture, a weather-worn monument, a self-sustaining spaceship unable to reach its pilot.

The laughter of the men found its way in through the bathroom window. Why did men always have to be so loud? I felt like I was back in college, hiding in the bathroom at a party and waiting for everyone to go away, for the world to rearrange itself into a place where I didn't have to hide and mark my face with something that made me need hiding.

I remembered then: Froyo kid. Theseus. The HE stamp, marked elegantly enough to reveal itself a habit.

I sat on the ugly teal countertop and took out my phone. It was kind of shitty to strand my mom, but it was also kind of shitty of her to ask me to come to these things. Not to mention that, at that point, I was rapidly approaching my mid-twenties, which meant the end to my extended adolescence by way of post-secondary education was nearing. My chances to be shitty were running out. I pulled up Theseus' number.

*Hey. It's me, from the other day. Can I ask you a question?*

I hit send, my gut churning with the anxiety that comes with anticipating a reply to a text message; like waiting for water to boil, except with way more potential for social repercussions. After a minute, the little dots tutted at the bottom of the screen, followed by his reply:

> *Froyo Dipz is hiring, but I respect you too much to let you apply. I know someone at that cursed games place who could probably score you a keyholder position. 16/hr!*

*Thanks, but it isn't about a job. It might be a personal
question actually? So don't feel like you have to answer if
it's too weird.*

> *Right on. What do you want to know?*

I hesitated. *I was just wondering about your HE stamp.*

> *What about it?*

Was he being difficult on purpose? I squirmed on the
countertop, trying not to be uncomfortable about a topic I had
broached myself.

*Like . . . why do you have it?*

It felt like he was typing forever, and while I knew that it
was pretty unlikely that I'd be hit with a five hundred character
scolding, I couldn't hold back the fear that I had misstepped
somehow. The way I saw it, questions like this were only
allowed to exist for as long as they weren't given a voice.

Women's laughter rang out from the yard, its brightness
nearly overpowering the endless onslaught of men's conversation. I was glad I was in the bathroom. It was nice to be invisible,
to engage the trusty cloaking mechanism. My phone lit up.

> *It's something I picked up when I was still living in the city.
> My roommate was a drag king, and they used to put on
> the HE-stamp in one of their acts as like . . . a cheeky (ha)
> commentary on stamps as tools of marginalization/ploys to sell
> more makeup? Idk they're a lot better at verbalizing this stuff.
> But I thought it was really cool, and I started wearing it myself.
> Why'd you ask? Thinking of abandoning your S?*

The question sent an unexpected jolt through my body, something like terror or yearning. My thumbs moved faster than my brain, inputting some easy, lazy reply:

*I've never noticed it when you're at Froyo Dipz.*

> *Yeah no way lol. Not looking to out myself to every clown looking for overpriced mall snacks. But like when I'm alone, or around people I trust or who I think are cool, it makes me feel good to wear it.*

*It doesn't remind you of the* SHE *stamp?* It was hard to imagine differentiating the two—ink was ink, wasn't it?

> *I mean, sort of? But also no. Like I'm a guy, I've almost always known that I'm a guy, but I wasn't raised as one, which makes my life experience fundamentally different from cis guys. So I use the stamp as a way of choosing masculinity for myself, but masculinity that isn't cis. Being a man on my own terms, I guess.*

I touched my cheek, considering what it would mean to treat masculinity or femininity as an option rather than a demand. To grant myself a little imagination, or something. Realistically, I understood the notion of gender presentation, that someone could be a woman without performing society's definition of femininity, and vice versa with men. And beyond that, I knew about trans people—the internet was a thing, and a couple old high school friends of mine had come out in the past few years. I marveled at their ability to know themselves, to identify where something wasn't working and act on the changes they needed to be happy. Envied it, even.

Theseus chose his version of masculinity, of *manhood*, every morning. What was I choosing? What decision was being made when I smeared on that word that became a name that became a way of life?

The phone lit up again.

> *Sorry—did any of that make sense??*

*No, yeah, I think I get it,* I typed back quickly.
*But follow-up: are you always so open with people?*

> *Eh. Depends on the person.*

*You hardly know me.*

> *Yeah but I have a good feeling. If I'm wrong, I'll be less trusting next time. Plus you despaired about capitalism in my car with your shirt off, so I felt like maybe I should do something to even things out.*

A laugh shot out of me. I leaned back against the mirror, feeling the cool contact of a reflection I did not intend on meeting. I thought about the light in his iris, the way he made me so curious in that shitty old car.

*Do you want to hang out?*

> *When?*

*I don't know. Tonight? I don't have a job.*

> *I'm off today, mostly just playing Stardew Valley. I could impress you with my many cows and my well-maintained vegetable garden. You could help me choose a cool wife.*

*Bet you say that to all the—*
(The what? The what?)
*—people you have over.*

            *Just the ones who ask personal questions. Need me to pick you up?*
*That would be great.*

And I guess that's how our whole thing began.

*Meanwhile, when the caring gets careless . . .*

The travelers do not realize they are being tailed until the B.O.D.Y. is boarded. It happens on the outskirts of a quiet colony on P-Unknown-43: a smooth voice, a false warrant, a tourist's welcome. The prince lets in the stranger, one of the semi-gaseous species called Czilokii, without a second thought, even as Bo's lights pulse uncertainly. The ship is running on low power, recharging for the evening; not the best time to welcome strangers. The rogue dismisses the worry—why would a small-time officer from far-off Czil wish him harm?

It does not take him long to realize his mistake. The moment Bo's doors close, the stranger pulls out the obsidian blade of a hired killer. The prince has seen them so many times in movies that some disbelieving part of him wonders if it's a prop—that is, until it arcs sharply in his direction.

He darts back from the weapon, and the assassin stalks him deeper into the ship. Behind him, a distant nebula glitters in the round window. To the stranger, this is nothing but a small job ordered by a big name for satisfactory payment. To the rogue, this is nothing but his life. Hadn't he been searching for danger? Wasn't that why he went on this adventure in the first place? Except he hadn't considered the implications for his ship, hadn't thought of all the scrappers out there that would love to get their hands on a unit like Bo. Faced with the idea that his B.O.D.Y. might be put in harm's way, destroyed and repurposed at the will of another, the prince hardens himself to fight.

"Stay back!" he shouts, grabbing a wrench from the toolbox. He swings it wildly, trying to keep the stranger back from Bo's core processing hub. He bares his teeth like an animal, refusing to let the scrapper touch his ship. "Who are you? What do you want?"

The stranger's physiology makes them move like a shadow, darting around him with disorienting speed. When they still, they pull up their warrant and let the pixels rearrange into a picture of honesty: a paid request for the death of the man that might be Cornelius Flux. The liar, the cheat. The spoiled prince. Do with him what you will. Eat him, if you'd like. Send him back to his family in pieces, if you so please.

"Is this—" The wrench seems to lower of its own volition, even as Bo's alarm screams scarlet all around him. He hears the beeping of programs executing and aborting faster than the prince can identify them. The prince cannot understand what he is being faced with. He does not have the self-preservation to know when people cannot be reasoned with. He is young, and does not believe he can die. "Is this about Lvrna?"

The assassin tilts their head, letting out a gruesome, steaming exhale that might be laughter. The rogue's grip on the wrench gives out when the obsidian blade darts in like a viper, splitting his forearm. He shouts in pain—he did not expect such a primitive weapon to hurt so terribly. He did not expect the warmth of the blood that falls from him.

"I'm not—" A boot to the chest sends his slight frame to the ground, choking on nothing. Above, Bo's lights are going wild, shouting directions that he cannot follow. The assassin crouches over him, amused pity on their face. The prince doesn't want to die.

The lights go dark.

A mechanical clang. A heavy thud, a gurgling groan. Wet iron, splattering down on the shaking prince. He waits, paralyzed by fear, but death does not come for him. When he finds his breath, the prince pulls himself out from under a body that does not move, that seems to hang suspended above him. What must be the assassin's blood stings against his skin, hissing as it dissolves into the air.

"Bo?" he calls, antennae twitching as he struggles to get his bearings in the complete blackness. He tries to open his throat eyes to read for heat signatures, but his panic keeps the thick lids clenched shut. "Bo, sweetheart, talk to me!" The talking lights stay down. Only the muted whirr of ylem remains, a comfort in the dark as the prince clutches his bleeding arm. He scootches back against the wall, seeking the comfort of his best and only friend.

"Bo?" he whispers, pressing his face to the paneling. He should do something, he should *move*, but he's frozen in place, trembling like a child. "Are you there? Bo, please say something. Please."

It feels like a very long time before the lights come up. The prince sees the assassin's body dangling in the center of the ship, skewered by six of Bo's grasps. Their blood sizzles on the floor while his own congeals, tacky violet on his arm. He feels lightheaded.

From above, a pop of light. Another. A stutter of communication.

The prince sobs in relief, kissing the ship's side paneling. "There you go, there you are. Take your time, it's okay. I'm with you, we're okay. We're okay."

The talking lights come in short bursts, the colors flickering rapid static.

"What?" The prince sits up, frightened. "What happened, where are you hurt?"

Bo's grasps pull out from the assassin with a horrible slick noise, the effort of the motion making the cabin's floor lights flicker. Instead of retreating into the ship's interior, the grasps hang limply in the cabin as the gore slowly dissipates. The assassin's body is in a heap on the floor, more disturbing for its stillness.

"I . . . I guess we're lucky that Czilokii guts don't linger, huh?" the prince laughs shakily. "Less work for—"

Bo's lights explode into a violent fuchsia that makes him flinch. Brightness roars through the ship, then slams back into darkness. The silence that follows fills the room with heaviness, tension that threatens to crack the air like chalk.

The prince cradles his arm, swallowing around the dryness in his throat, trying to backtrack. "No, I mean, I get it's in the air circulation, but it's not, you know—"

The lights spark patternless, strong enough to blow out a string of talking bulbs. The prince has never seen his B.O.D.Y. unit like this before. Then again, he has never seen someone die inside of it. He softens his voice.

"It's inside of you," he echoes back, closing his eyes. "I hear you. I can't imagine how that feels. I'm sorry."

The ship pulses affirmative after affirmative, but its systems don't regulate. The temperature is dropping, the cabin lights cannot sustain themselves.

"Thank you for saving me—" the prince begins, but the talking lights silence him again, frantic and venomous. Tangerine shocks so loudly through the cabin that the prince jumps, taking in the meaning at a nauseating pace:

*How dare how dare you you said it was okay just a game just okay Bo worries too much B.O.D.Y. nags and nags you liar Cornelius I am so I am so I am so so so*

Cornelius knows that now is a good time to listen instead of talk, but his arm hurts and he is afraid and he bristles at the ship's accusations. "I wasn't trying to lie about Lvrna! I just didn't think it would go so far, I didn't think—no, shut up! Listen to me! I should have told you, I get that now, but you're acting like I did this intentionally. It was a mistake, but we're both safe now! You saved us!"

The grasps shoot out in front of the prince's face, the force of the motion dimming the ship's lights. He freezes, watching the last of the viscera crumbling away, getting pulled into the air Bo will recycle for him to breathe. They'll need a full cleanout. A wave of dizziness washes over him. He wants to press his forehead to the floor.

Above him, the talking lights move nearly too fast for the prince to keep up with. It hurts his eyes to watch, but he does not dare look away from Bo's fury, its grief. He holds himself steady and bears witness to this pain of his own making. The ship's ceiling performs its emotions like a firework display, relentless.

"I'll . . . I'll take care of the body," he says when floor lights calm, when the temperature stabilizes. His fingers feel stuck to his forearm; he's afraid if he pulls them away that he might just tear apart. That doesn't make him so different from Bo, really. "This is my mess, I won't just shove it onto you. I'm sorry you had to . . . to do that. To save me. To kill them. That wasn't fair."

A string of bulbs glow and quiet like a falling star, interrupted by the filaments that blew out in the ship's distress. The prince winces. "You're not a weapon. Or an afterthought or a, a *sidekick*. You're my friend! You're my friend, Bo. I love you. I love you so much that it hurts. I don't know what to do with myself."

The lights warm imploringly, insistently. It is a plea and a challenge and a demand:

*Figure it out, Cornelius. For both of us, figure something out.*

*vi.*

We played a lot of Stardew Valley in the weeks after that.

Theseus had a small studio apartment in one of the high rises near the town's major train station. Like everyone else who lived here, he had this long term plan of moving into the city, but also like everyone else who lived here, he realized that the price of living downtown was pretty much entirely unattainable. Rent for his place was low, and the pay at Froyo Dipz was surprisingly high. Apparently some ancient corporate drama had gotten him accidentally promoted to manager a few years back, and the responsibilities weren't too bad in the mall's off-season. When he wasn't ordering frozen cheesecake bites and wearing a degrading hat, he had plenty of time to do what he cared about.

Mostly, he cared about making bizarre, ambient little video games that he shared on a very niche forum and sometimes sold for actual money. He had played a lot of games over the years, but the stuff he personally developed could best be described as an unholy chimera of interactive arthouse media. I'd spent a lot of my life tolerating musicians and being exhausted by poets, so it was nice to be introduced to a new form of expression, even if I didn't always get what he was going for.

"I couldn't really keep up with journaling," he said one

day as he adjusted a new game's textures. "But I needed to do something to feel a little less crazy. I used to just play games all the time, really obsessively. I wanted to get lost in a story, get out of this world that I didn't know how to exist in. And I guess it worked—but then I sort of lost *myself*, too. So I started making these to try and find me again."

"Did you?"

"I guess so. I mean, I'm here, right?" His sheepish smile said that hadn't always been a given. "Even though they kind of ate my life for a while, I'm still grateful for the games. They really helped me to figure myself out, to—"

"Customize your character?"

"Oh my God. You're the worst." The despairing awe in his voice was a new world wonder. "But yeah, totally."

He walked me through a few of his projects. We played a couple favorite games of his, mostly super choice-based RPGs where he'd gently nudge me toward the answers that would get me what I wanted. At his insistence, we played a post-apocalyptic dating sim where we pursued pigeons as romanceable options. It was incredibly bizarre. It was fantastic.

But Stardew Valley was our home base—it didn't take much thought or effort to pass the days, the weeks, the seasons. As we raised our chickens and gave flowers to our neighbors and conspired to take down corporate evil, we talked. About books and family, far-fetched dreams and existential terror. I couldn't remember the last time I'd connected with a new friend. Honestly, the painful retreat from university and those years I gave to selling mediocre lotion lost me a lot of people that I cared about. I was a pretty self-sustaining animal, easily tired by crowds and happy to spend days on end with a stack of books, but it felt good to remember what it was like to have someone who tried to get me, and who I tried to get in return.

So one day, after we finally fixed up the pantry in the Community Center and hyped up the junimo, I kissed him. There wasn't much time to worry about how he'd respond— the contact of our mouths triggered a vision of him standing in an art gallery, wiping his eyes. And then I was present again, and he was kissing me back, the controller pushed to the side as I found my way into his lap.

It had been a long time since I kissed anyone, and Theseus was not shy. In everything else he was laid back, a little uncertain, but he was bold in his wanting. Apparently farming RPGs built up a lot of unresolved tension.

When we finally paused long enough to do that Hollywood heavy-breathing-eye-contact thing, I watched the crease of doubt return to his face. I recognized the look, the classic worry that comes after a first kiss, the fear that somehow one act of physicality will manage to change the fundamentals of a relationship. The exhausted fear of losing what you had by acting on only one part of what you wanted.

I was trying to figure out how to explain how much I didn't want that to happen when I looked over his shoulder at the television screen. "Dude!"

"What?"

"You didn't pause?!"

"Oh shit—"

"We just lost like four hours!" I shouted. "And we still need to get Clint that fucking iron!"

He all but shoved me to the side, grabbing at the controller and cursing. His face was flushed and his hair was a mess, but he seemed genuinely concerned about our pickaxe upgrade. That was what encouraged me to explain later that I wasn't looking for a serious relationship. It was easier for me to share my body, harder for me to share my life. He didn't mind. He seemed relieved, even.

So thus began our hobbies: hooking up and playing video games. I know that I got another job at some point, that my life went on outside of our bounty of save data and Theseus' studio apartment. But when I think back to that part of my life, when I was working my way out of being a girl, this was what mattered. This is what stayed: tender words from computer programs, pizza coupons pillaged from the building's recycling bins, Theseus' breath stuttering as I played with his T-dick, my own fits of post-orgasmic laughter.

One rainy day, as the giggles faded to normal breathing, my fingers found themselves tracing the scars on Theseus' chest, old grave-markers. They were shiny against the pale matte of his skin, like the insides of seashells, smooth to the touch. To my relief, this particular moment of contact didn't trigger any visions. It was nice, being allowed a moment to be *in* the moment.

Theseus passed me the mug of water that was dubiously balanced on the headboard, reaching for a towel that had been thrown on the floor. "It's remarkable, how quickly you manage to shove me into the wet spot."

"If you were less gifted with the strap, it wouldn't be such an issue."

"Well *that* isn't going to happen," he said with a theatrical sigh. "Guess it's my burden to bear."

"Guess so." I took a long sip of water, watching as Theseus loosened the harness around his hips. The cock attached was purple and glittery and perfectly thick, our go-to when Theseus was feeling playful. Otherwise, we swapped out with the more realistic alternative he kept in what was lovingly called 'the sin box.'

This might sound weird, but those hyper-transitory moments when we prepared the tools of the trade were nearly sacred to me. No matter how much my mom preached a culture of consent, the world around me had still enforced this idea that choices weren't really choices, that things just happened and it was best to roll with it. But sex with Theseus was a series of questions and preparations, every pause an opportunity to be present. *You cool with this? How do you want me to fuck you? You like that? Do you want more? Will you take it for me? Fuck, you're gorgeous.*

Maybe it was all that open communication that made it so easy to stumble into what came next.

I was rubbing at my SHE stamp, trying to get an idea of how smeared it was—Theseus' *he* was halfway to his ear. His slim fingers were tucked beneath the straps, exposing gentle lines imprinted on his skin. As with most fateful things, the question I asked was more of an impulse than anything: "What does it feel like?"

"Hm?"

"The strap-on."

He laughed. "You tell me."

"No, that's not—" I shoved at him, laughing a little even as something electric tingled at the base of my skull. "I mean like . . . how does it feel for you?"

Theseus paused for a moment, consideration furrowing his brow. He cracked a smile, shrugging a little. "I dunno. It's . . . really good? Makes me feel more like me, sometimes, if that makes sense. Character customization and all that."

"But I mean, do you feel . . ." I trailed off, feeling lost. When Theseus was fucking me with the toy, he looked as hungry and breathless as any cis guy I'd ever had sex with. When I wrapped my hand around whatever cock he was wearing, he reacted like he'd been born with it attached. It was unreal to watch. It made something ache in me. "Sorry. I don't really know what I'm asking."

"Do you want to try it?" he asked.

"What?" Another electrical impulse.

"My cock. Do you want to try it on?" The words came out so easily, like it was just some simple idea that didn't make me feel like I was swimming through some wildly psychedelic river. Back then, an offer like this felt unspeakably dangerous. My fluid sexuality was a creature I had long since built a home with, but my longing for gender security was unknown terrain. I knew my body as a conduit of desire, an experience best shared with others.

But when it was just me and a mirror, me and my fingers, me and a long night awake playing out stories of runaway rogues and lonely motherships and unbelonging behind my eyes . . . I felt like an amalgamation of parts that didn't quite fit, a chaotic scrap pile of body and mind.

"Yeah," I said, trying very hard to act like my chest wasn't full of terror and still water. "Yeah, I'll try."

After some finagling with straps, Theseus helped me into the apparatus that made him feel more like himself when we fucked. I wasn't sure how I felt about it. Looking down at the sparkling strangeness protruding from me felt alien, almost laughable. I wiggled, watching it bob, and tried to understand the appeal. The cock always made sense when I saw it on Theseus, but on me it felt like writing with the wrong hand.

I almost asked Theseus to help me take it off, but then he grinned at me, goofy and sincere. "It looks great!"

"Don't make fun of me," I said, pulling the dildo back and watching it bounce. At least it was entertaining.

"I'm not!" he insisted, kissing me. "It looks cool. You don't think so?"

"It looks . . ." I bit his lip, smiling as he hummed in response. "Purple. Really purple."

"The sexiest color," he nodded, working his mouth down my neck. I could feel the strap-on pushing against his belly. I liked the firmness of it, the way it pressed back against my pubic bone.

"Was there a vote?" I asked. "Because I must have missed—"
He stole the words from me with his grasping fingers, his wanting tongue. Theseus had so much want in him, and I loved the way it inspired my own. We hadn't even had a chance to power up any of his consoles today before my back hit the mattress.

I pulled him back up for another kiss, wishing I could pull the soul right out of him. Sex always brought out chaos in me. Made me feel kind of vulnerable and violent and apart from myself, but also with myself too. Like a ship never quite touching ground, a hair's breadth from all unyielding earth. The engine in me burned. Theseus climbed on top of me, bringing his mouth back to my neck, my chest, my belly. He bit, and I arched my back, the (his? (my?)) cock nudging his chest.

"Can I show you something?" he asked quietly, lips brushing the strap-on. I didn't breathe. I nodded. I needed.

The moment before his tongue touched the head, the world seemed to slow down. My eyes have always had this habit of going cinematic in the face of oncoming epiphany, and this was no exception. The walls warped like we were underwater, our bodies smooth and retouched to reflect the realities of a stacked multiverse. I floated, watching Theseus' kiss-swollen lips, his hollowed cheeks. My hands found their way to his hair, pushing it back so I could see more of his face.

The vision came on lazily—Theseus on a phone call, laughing and saying a name I did not recognize but knew to be my own. I couldn't take it in fully, so desperate was I for the present. There's something surreal about watching someone swallow down a part of you. That's how it felt then, like that ridiculous purple cock was a part of me, perfect and glittering.

"I—" I what? What? Theseus hummed around the silicone in a way that might have been sympathetic, pressing a hand into my hip.

The sounds he was making were obscene, and I trembled as I remembered how this new part of me had been inside me not a half hour before. I turned outside in, inside out; the assembled body, reimagined to something fluid and mutable. Theseus pulled back, licking the shaft as he reached between my legs, slipping his fingers into me. He pumped them to the rhythm of his sucking, displacing me from all sense of physicality. My fingers twisted in his hair, my hips lifted, pushing my cock further into his mouth, urging his fingers deeper.

I was a shapeshifter, worshipped for my pluralities. Without, within. So many stories of self, huddled together to wander the void of my own uncertainty, fleeing and seeking in equal measure. Transcendent. The lights within me spoke an impossible language, and all at once the ship of my body caught a proper glimpse of its lonesome occupant.

Lilac skin, velvet coat, the many eyes that would not look back at me. More a symbol than a boy, a rogue collection of drifting thoughts. Back then, I didn't really know him well— what he wanted, what he *was*. But I loved him just the same.

When orgasm hit, I thought I would drown. I didn't, obviously. But I thought I would, and so I cried like I had just tasted the first breath of my life.

Theseus held me, and I was thankful. His body was warm and his voice was gentle, and he didn't try to make me stop crying. I closed my eyes as I took deep shuddering breaths, searching for the afterimages that had been left by this new state of being. Searching for one more look at the creature who lived within me, who I carried so tenderly through this life and could not reach, could not touch, could not yet understand.

*Where are you?* I asked myself. From my heart, a mechanical hum.

*What are you?* I asked myself. From my head, a rogue's whispered wanting.

*Why is this happening?* I asked myself. *Why is this happening to me?*

Silence, silence. Perfect and terrible. The sympathetic resonance of the great dark universe, waiting to be heard.

*I don't know if you remember this. We were so young.*

The prince sat alone by the lake, those many years ago. He was hiding, though he can no longer remember what from; he was crying too, though he can no longer remember why. Many afternoons were spent this way, looking out at the rippling pink waters and trying to understand where and when and how he was. Everything was too big, and he could not find his place in it, and his words all came out too loud or too quiet.

This is what most people call childhood. From what the prince has been told, it's something that's meant to be looked back on fondly.

But the prince does not think he knew what happiness was, before Bo.

That day, as he wept into his knees, the B.O.D.Y. unit came over to investigate. It was so new back then, metallic casing around an unrefined lump of ylem, no larger than a toaster, with a single blinking bulb that could answer yes or no questions.

But Bo did not answer anyone's questions, before Cornelius.

Eager to investigate this small organic, it flew up to the boy too quickly, bumping him on the forehead. He shouted and fell back, his face all snot and distressed hiccuping. He stared at the small machine, antennae twitching in alarm. "Who are you?" he asked, both sets of eyes gone wide.

The B.O.D.Y. said nothing, unsure of how to respond.

"What do you want?" the boy whimpered, rubbing his eyes. Machines couldn't laugh at people for crying, could they? He hated being laughed at.

The B.O.D.Y. said nothing, unsure of how to respond.

The boy looked around nervously. Did this strange, flying thing belong to anyone? He picked himself up off the ground, cautiously examining the machine for any sigils or signatures. It bobbed in front of him, the whir of its engine barely audible over the song of the cicadas, the splash of silvery beasts that roamed the deep end of the lake.

"Are you . . . are you a B.O.D.Y.?" he asked shyly.

The robot gave a single, bright blink of its bulb, pleased to have been asked a question it could understand.

"Wow!" The prince had heard of these before—Bionic Organic Developmental Ylem! Sentient machines powered by life-giving cores, able to assemble their parts the same way organics picked out clothing or exoshells. They were mostly nomadic, traveling where they wished until they took an interest in something long enough to form a bond. No one really knew where they came from, or what they wanted from other sentient species. "Do you have a name?"

The B.O.D.Y.'s light flickered a low negative.

"Can I give you one?"

The bulb brightened, cautious—

"Is Bo okay?"

—and grew brighter still, happy to have been named by this soft, tearful thing. The boy's palms were wide and clumsy, his fingers pudgy and curious as he kneaded at his pants. Even a unit as new as this B.O.D.Y., as new as *Bo*, could see that he wanted to touch. It's in the nature of organics, to grab when they get curious. Bo flew around him, bumping at his arms, wanting to be the first to initiate contact.

The boy laughed, hugging himself. The B.O.D.Y. thought it was the loveliest sound, and nudged him until he reached out, resting a hand on its outer paneling. He marveled at its clever design, tried to envision what shape it would build for itself. Riverboat, mecha-mole, floating museum? Mobile home, self-cycle, spaceship? It fluttered so gracefully, he thought. It would make a beautiful spaceship.

"Will you be my friend, Bo?" he asked. His eyes were wide and hopeful, his heart alight with longing. The unit was warm beneath his touch, its soul-engine humming with want of its own.

The B.O.D.Y. loved him from the start. Its light grew stronger, testing the bulb, aspiring to match the suns. How else could it show the boy that it would be there for him always, that it would travel with no other? How else could it make their first meeting flare bright enough that neither of them could ever lose it, or distort it in their memories?

Things were so easy in their youth, when they each ached only for an anchor. Life was so simple, when all they had to fear was everything but each other. Home was such a comfort, back when being understood felt more a purpose than a plague.

It is easy to grieve the way things change, to get crushed beneath the uncertainty of what they could become. So let us, for a moment, give thanks for beginnings; for two young wanderers, new to the world and a little afraid, choosing each other. Choosing to belong.

Belonging even still, though they cannot yet remember how.

I fell pretty hard down an internet rabbit hole after the whole cosmic cock-sucking epiphany. Well, no, first I had a panic attack. It started not too long after I detached myself from Theseus and excused myself to go pee, which is only best practice. I had stopped crying, which was as good as permission to move on.

*I'm okay!* I told myself. *That was extremely weird and life-changing, but my life doesn't have to change! Everything is okay and exactly the same and I am fine!*

But the thing about being stuck alone in a small room after having an otherworldly out-of-body experience is that it really doesn't lend itself to a sense of normalcy. I stared down at my toes, curling and uncurling them, feeling embodied to the point of ghastliness. Then I thought about the strap-on, and how it felt so much like a part of me, which was wild because it was just a conveniently-shaped piece of silicone. And then I remembered this episode of one of those *Betcha Don't Know Where Anything In Your Daily Life Comes From, Dipshit!* shows, and how it explained that silicone just comes from silica and fossil fuels and human effort, and then I was thinking about fossil fuels and dinosaurs and all those years they spent turning to goo in the ground just to end up in my vagina and wasn't that sick and when I die whose vagina will I end up in and oh god I'm going to die I'm dying every moment I'm alive I am just waiting to die and rot and maybe eventually end up back in someone's vagina—

Looking back, it's kind of funny. Circle of life, right? But back then, when I was splashing water on my face and trying to remember how to breathe, it felt as though I had come completely unmoored from all sense of self. I faced my reflection in the mirror and found my cheek *she*-less, the stamp rubbed away by sweat and saliva and tears. I reached out, pressing my fingers to the glass, and swore something else reached out to touch me back. A robotic grasp where a hand should be.

Maybe that sounds crazy. It felt a little crazy, even though it's also mostly true.

Theseus was really good about the whole thing. He rubbed my back when I got sick, saying things about gender dysphoria and complicated feelings and experiences being valid and so on. His voice sounded very far away, but I tried my best to listen. Self-discovery is a lonely experience by definition, but I don't think it has to be done alone.

When I calmed down, we ate some mediocre frozen spanakopita thing, and he drove me home. I promised I'd text if I needed him, and he promised he wouldn't treat me like I was fragile just because I had an extraordinarily bizarre reaction to the best sex of my life. My mom was out with friends, so it was easy to slip into the house and lock myself in my room.

Enter: the rabbit hole.

I have a complicated relationship with the internet. It's supposed to be this magical, unlimited resource, this space for strangers all across the world to come together in the name of shared information. Mostly it's full of cat videos and porn, but maybe that's not a bad thing either, to want to laugh and get off between learning *everything*. Because that's the part where things start to fall apart: I get online, and I find the answers I was looking for, but I also get more than that. The screen's bright and shiny, and information demands more information, and suddenly I know more than I ever wanted or asked for with approximately zero idea of how to process any of it.

Curled up on my bed with my laptop overheating on my knees, answers came to me like so many stones around my neck. My search terms looked like a toddler's garbled questioning, unintelligible for all their sincerity.

*Not a boy or girl*

> *History of SHE stamps women who don't wear stamps*
>> *who aren't women?*

*How do I know if I'm not a woman but not a man*

> *Gender isn't anything but also is something*

> *History of space flight*

> *Future of space flight*

*Do I have to have a gender to go to space?*

> *Dysphoria definition*

> *Transgender definition*

*Why do some people write trans\* with a little star?*

> *Closest stars to Earth that aren't the sun*

As the panic rose in me, I searched for a story to tell myself. Something about a galaxy far away where gender didn't mean anything and a body was just a means of navigation. Fictionalizing my life and my emotions was an old strategy. It was the fastest way to streamline my processing, to shape my experience into something I actually wanted to look at. Only this time, it wasn't working.

I couldn't claim my body a spaceship without facing the pilot. Keeping a safe distance was impossible when every answer to every question had a direct, immediate impact on my life.

Every word Wikipedia turned up had to be applied to myself: *nonbinary, genderqueer, genderfluid, agender, bigender.* Answers only led to more questions, and questions only led to more self-investigation, and all the dissociative metaphors I had couldn't protect me from the fact that something had fundamentally changed within me.

Well, no, I don't know if *changed* is the right word. It had always been there. But now I was looking at it, and more importantly, it was looking back.

It had more eyes than I expected.

I covered my face, breathing slowly like I was back in that child therapist's room. I remembered the colorful foam mats, the enormous spider plant that I used to be afraid of because I thought it was where spiders came from. I focused on the face of my therapist, her big artsy earrings and her polka dot stamp and her nails like perfect talons. What would she say to me?

*Oh, She, honey, it's okay to be confused. It makes sense that you would be thinking about this stuff so critically—you're a very bright young girl!*

I felt myself small and shaking, full of childish anguish and helpless terror. What would I say back?

*I'm not, though.*

*Not bright? Don't be silly!*

*No. I'm not a girl. I'm not a girl.*

*I'm sorry, I'm so sorry, I'm not a girl.*

The confession came in a burst of brilliant light, supernova of honesty long overdue, and then went dark. I grasped at my body with shaking hands, trying to keep myself from malfunctioning, falling from the sky into a million unfixable pieces.

My phone buzzed sympathetic death throes at the foot of my bed. I plugged it in, considered calling Theseus. He was one of the only people I knew who had experience with gender anxiety, definitely the only one I felt close enough with to ask questions. In this small town, I knew I was lucky to have anyone to talk to at all. But something old and stubborn calcified in my fingers.

My grandmother's voice, this time. Remade from the stardust blessing of her memory.

*A strong woman like you doesn't need to rely on a man. They think they're so clever, but they don't know a thing. You'll find your answers in yourself, or else ask the other women in your life. They'll have the sense to put you on the right track!*

If I wasn't a woman, did the logic still apply? And Theseus was very much a man, but we'd talked a bunch of times about what it meant to be transmasculine versus your standard common or garden variety cis guy, so did that mean I could talk to him? I could feel the expectation of my family's sacred counterculture, the pressure of womanhood bearing down on my chest. I didn't like it, but I wasn't so sure what it would mean to release it. If men were unreliable and women were no longer accessible to me, where was I supposed to go?

I tossed my phone aside, gave in to faulty logic: if I could find a way through this without any help, I could claim to know what I was doing even a little bit. Back down the rabbit hole I went.

Hours passed. Hours of blog posts and definitions and academic articles, TEDx talks and vloggers and video essays. I learned the language, gained a sense of story. I scrolled through before and after images of people's coming out stories, gazed into their smiling faces. Theys and xes and zes, as both and neither and in-between as I apparently was. Nonbinary.

*Affirming,* they said. *Coming out was an incredibly affirming experience. It was scary, but it felt good to finally be myself.*

I burned. I hurt. I did not feel affirmed.

This is the part of the story that I'm always so tempted to revise. Who doesn't want their epiphany to be joyful? Who doesn't want to look back on self-discovery with pride? These days, I'm so glad to be who and what I am, hatched and whole. So I wish I could tell you that back then, my discovery of other stories, other possible futures, felt like an exciting thing, like the first step in a beautiful process. But it didn't. Not at first.

For someone who had struggled against boundaries my whole life, I sure fell apart without structure. University had felt impossible, but the eternal summer that was adulthood was outright paralyzing. The concept of marriage felt like a nightmare, but the dating world was a true screeching hell. The laws of gender felt suffocating, but the bounty of *no rules* identity formation made me feel hollow, hungry for answers I did not know how to discover for myself, let alone explain to others.

I wasn't like Theseus. I wasn't sorted into Box A instead of Box B at birth—I fell off the assembly line altogether. Most people in this shitty little suburban town didn't even know what a binary was. No matter what I did, they would just choose to see me as a woman. So why not hide? Why make things harder? Why should I have to come out again when I already did the queer thing? Why should I have to be new to myself, to reintroduce myself to a world that would gladly reject me?

Back then, compared to my anxiety, happiness felt like such a small thing. It was hard to think of a world where things could get better, so focused I was on maintaining a life where it didn't get worse.

I pushed up my sleeves, feeling the pulse of blood beneath my skin, the brush of the fine hairs on my forearms. I closed my eyes, reaching for my visions, searching for the futures hidden in my being. All my life, I had been blessed with the luxury of seeing outcomes. Once I knew what was coming, I could make the right choices.

My own skin hadn't ever initiated a vision before. I don't know why I thought it would start now, but I *wanted*. For a moment, I was struck with terror at the thought that maybe all my visions were gone now, gone forever, because I had faced the fact that I could not be a woman. That I didn't know if I'd ever been a girl at all.

"Please," I prayed to the things I couldn't even name, the things that had apparently made me what I was but didn't have the good grace to let me in on the secret. "Please."

I sat there for a long time, clutching at my own skin. It felt as though I had just discovered my entire life had been spent in a cocoon. I scratched at its soft edges, the papery surface of my perceived world, but I could not break through. I did not know how. I did not dare.

*Meanwhile, on a vast and hungry world . . .*

The prince and his ship enter the atmosphere of the planet Nameless, a world blanketed in coniferous trees grown so close together that their roots and branches are permanently entangled. From above, it looks like a vast green ocean, and the prince wonders at its depth, its depths. Leagues of verdant life.

Bo struggles at first to find a good place to land. The ship has never been the sort to plow through other organisms for the sake of convenience. It hovers just above the treeline, searching until it eventually comes across a small clearing near a great, still lake. It hums uncomfortably at the sight of the dark waters, but the prince is unconcerned. He grew up near a lake himself.

Bo pops its talking bulbs warily, hesitant to touch down.

"It looks fine to me, Bo," the prince says. He can hear how clipped his tone is, and it frustrates him. He brushes it off as exhaustion—they've had a long flight, Bo's being picky, and he wants to taste air that hasn't been recycled. "Just a lake."

He flicks through the navigation screen, pulling up the limited information on record about Nameless. It is a remote planet, with few resources the major galactic forces consider worth pillaging. Aside from a few scientific ventures, it has, for the most part, been left well enough alone. The prince likes the sound of that; some of the greatest thinkers of the homeworld have sung the praises of getting away from it all, of sitting somewhere quiet with your thoughts and listening in for the whisper of the universe.

It's been hard to hear anything over the static of his own thoughts, lately. Some time on Nameless seems like a good remedy.

"Give it another look if you like," he says, closing the screen. "But last we checked, the flora's pretty solid cover for anyone searching out life. It'll disorient their own scanners, same as yours. It's a good spot to lay low."

Not that they need to anymore. When the prince disposed of the assassin's body, he marked the death warrant as complete and collected payment. It makes him sick to carry the credits, but the person who sent out the hit would get suspicious if the assassin hadn't accepted the transfer.

As Bo reluctantly touches down upon the soft earth, the prince changes into something easy and lightweight, trying to relieve the pressure he feels building within his chest. He steps out of the ship, his feet moving seemingly of their own volition. When did his ship become such a claustrophobic place? When did it become so uncomfortable to be looked at by his best friend, his home?

Behind him, Bo's feet dig into the soil, stabilizing itself as a sturdy shelter. The prince breathes in the heady flavor of this hyper-oxygenated world. It makes him a little dizzy; he'll probably have to investigate the med box for something that'll help his body calibrate. The last thing he needs is to test his lungs this far from civilization.

Nameless is beautiful, though. Peaceful. The lake looks

thick as porridge, but maybe that's just a trick of the light. He wonders if he can go fishing in it, wonders what the fish might look like after spending their lives in such opaque waters.

It is so different from the silky rosé lake of his youth, and yet he cannot shake the way his mind wanders back to the homeworld. He aches for it, unexpectedly. He longs for his family, his friends, the familiar foods and the ornate walls that used to feel so tight and unyielding around him. He was not happy there, but he knew what to expect.

The prince presses his palms to the lower eyes on his throat. So much for the spirit of adventure.

He thought the space from his family would make it easier to understand the cosmic disorientation that's plagued him since childhood. Leaving was supposed to change things for the better; it was supposed to bring him closer to Bo, and to whatever version of himself he was apparently aiming for. Yet here he is, homesick and sorry.

It doesn't help that no one from home has contacted him in weeks and weeks. He doesn't know what's changed; when he first left, he was bombarded with messages. Worry from his mothers, playful goading from his friends, pleas from potential betrotheds, ads for local party venues. Then one day they stopped, and he had been too caught up in his head to worry about it.

Has everyone forgotten about him? Are they happy he's gone? Just because he needed to get away doesn't mean that he was looking to be left behind. If the price of finding himself is being abandoned, without even Bo for comfort . . .

Unless, of course, he hasn't been abandoned. The prince is

struck with the cold realization that it is very possible that they believe he is dead, especially considering the confirmation he just sent to the man who put a hit on him.

There it is again—that pressure in his chest. The prince presses his hands to his heart, breathing slowly; he'll be no good to anyone hyperventilating on the ground. He listens to the sounds of Bo running its security programs and tries to pull himself together. He needs to contact his family.

Space is such a possible thing, so vast and unknowable that truth is often lost, welcoming speculation in its place. If everyone thinks Cornelius Flux dead, then he's dead. And he is not ready to die. Not like this. Not alone and afraid.

The prince stumbles back into the ship, opening up the messaging screen and flicking through his empty inbox. What can he say to them, this family that has left him to the wild? It is perfect retaliation, he thinks, for the pleasure he took in leaving them. It isn't fair. None of the rogues in the stories ever struggle like this, no one ever told him that it was so damned *complicated* just to exist—

The prince finds something strange. All around him, Bo's bulbs pulse softly, nervously. It does not dare raise its voice.

The messages are tucked in a tidy, private folder. Out of sight from anyone but the desperate or the curious. Numbly, the prince scrolls through them, not even stopping to read the words on the screen. Kindness and worry, reminders of his place of origin in the universe.

"You've been hiding my messages . . . ?" He doesn't know why this comes out as a question. The answer is right here, isn't it?

The ship offers a timid affirmative. It makes the prince furious. What does Bo possibly have to be scared of? Bo can do everything, anything, it runs just *fine* whether or not he's there—he's just the straggler, come along for the journey. What right does the ship have?

"You've—" He runs a hand through his hair, feeling his fingers catch in the tangle of curls. The tug in his scalp brings him fully to himself, to his grief. "I thought that I was, that they didn't—I thought that no one *wanted* me Bo, can you even—"

Bo offers an anxious stripe of light, a meteorite of color, all burned up: *I want you, Cornelius. I love you, I wanted to keep you safe—*

The prince is out the door. The ship calls something after him, but he is running now, pushing his body through the dense wood. It is not enough to be loved, he realizes. It is not enough to be loved when you are not also trusted. How can he and Bo trust each other after what they have put each other through? How can they ever go back to where they began when they have strayed so far?

The prince loses himself to his fury, loses himself on the planet Nameless with its great many trees. The oxygen fills him with a foggy tranquility, an absent sense of despair. He feels the scratch of bark against his exposed forearms, takes in the sweet smell of tree sap. Vaguely, he gets the sense that something is wrong, but he figures it is something within rather than without. Isn't that how it's always been? He gives himself to the woods, fitting the arch of his foot to fallen pine cones, and he lets himself feel very sorry indeed.

But he does not notice the silence. Miles and miles of trees, home to all manner of life, and not a single sound.

Eventually, my mom started to worry. That shouldn't have been surprising; she's always been a good parent, attentive without being overbearing. There wasn't much I could get past her, so I found it was just easier to tell the truth and work through whatever small fallout might come from it. The only real conflict in our relationship came from the rare times when I tried lying to her.

My friends said that I was lucky to have a mother who actually listened to me. It was rare to have someone who was willing to do difficult work and compromise, who didn't just blow up for the thrill of re-enacting their childhood trauma.

Call it selfish, but I didn't feel lucky then.

"*She*?" my mom called through the door, knocking quietly. "Still breathing in there?"

"Still breathing," I answered.

"Can I come in? I brought fries."

I looked around at the hovel that was my room: the veritable rug of dirty clothing on the floor, the menagerie of mugs and water glasses, the power cord dragged closer so I wouldn't have to get out of bed to charge my phone. It looked like Barbie's Dream Depression House. Now that I thought of it, the only time I'd left this spot in the past couple days was to go to work, and that was its own special kind of timeless void.

This wasn't how I wanted my mother to find me. But I was too old to shout at her to go away. Even if I couldn't be a woman, I still had to be an adult.

"Fries sound good," I said, combing through my hair with my fingers. There was no salvaging my appearance, but it felt good to pretend for a minute.

To her credit, my mom did her best to contain her wince at the sight of my room. She had lived with me during depressive episodes before, so this wasn't entirely unfamiliar territory. But it was still frightening for her. What halfway decent parent doesn't have a private burst of panic at the sight of their kid visibly deteriorating under the weight of existence?

"Bad week?" she asked, stepping over my empty laundry basket, a bag of horrible fast food fries in her hand. I'd never smelled anything so good.

"You could say that." I reached out like a toddler, making grabby hands at the greasy paper bag.

"You know, one of my biggest parenting mistakes was giving you fast food at a young age." She passed the fries over and started foraging through the valley of mugs. "I know I was still a baby myself, but I could have done better. I good as poisoned you, got you hooked on the garbage—"

"Mom," I groaned, stuffing a salty fistful into my mouth.

"—and I know it's gotten better as you've gotten older, and more conscious of corporate greed and the environmental impact, but I still feel terrible that I ever exposed you to it in the first place."

"If you hate the stuff so much, why bring it?" I ate the fries faster, as though a bizarro version of my mother would suddenly appear and pull them away from me to teach me a lesson about hubris.

"Because you're in a self-destructive funk," she said, piling my clothing into the laundry basket. It felt a little easier to breathe, seeing the floor again. I didn't even have it in me to get all self-pitying about how difficult it was to do myself. "And if I offer too much support, you'll turn me away. So I figure if I poison you a little while I help tidy your room, you might be willing to talk to me about what's going on."

The knife of anxiety cut through the illusion of comfort another human and a mouthful of salt had brought on. All of the internet resources had said that it would be best to come out at my own pace, that living with a sort of performative, functional gender was perfectly valid if it was what it took to keep me safe. But I *was* safe already; my mother was a good person, she wasn't one of those monsters who would turn her back on her kid if she didn't like the way they were turning out.

This wasn't danger. It was just fear.

"It might sound kind of weird," I said, immediately regretting the way my voice betrayed my hesitation.

"I raised you," she said simply. "You've been weird before, *She*. I think I'll find a way to manage."

My name sounded so heavy in the air, predictive and dangerous. I ate another fry, trying to stop time. It didn't work.

"I don't think I'm a woman," I said.

"What?" She paused her tidying, looking me up and down

with a quirk of a smile. "Has something happened since I last changed your diapers?"

The joke hollowed me, made all the bulbs in my chest go abruptly dark. I looked at the stamp on her face, so proud and neat. A symbol of her strength, her creativity. I felt my face's own nakedness, and I wished suddenly that it had been intentional. That I hadn't just been curled up in a depression hole.

"That's not—" I glanced over at my laptop. "That's not really what I mean."

"So what do you mean?"

I was struck with the same nausea that comes when you share your favorite music with someone, the looming dread that maybe they'll hate this thing that's so meaningful. Or, more accurately, that upon listening together, you'll realize it was never actually that good in the first place. The grotesque lovechild of protectiveness and shame.

"It's sort of complicated . . ." Everything I'd read suddenly seemed so unintelligible. My laptop was right beside me, there was no reason I couldn't literally hand it over to the professionals, but I didn't want to. If I was going to commit to this new truth of myself, I wanted to at least be able to talk about it. I started from the beginning, combing through everything I had learned. My mom was a smart person, and progressive. She'd probably want the whole picture. "It's like, yes so I was born female—wait, no, I was assigned female at, at birth. I was born with a vagina, so people said I was a girl. But that's, I mean gender's socially constructed and stuff, but I guess it's feeling kind of—weird?"

"Do you not want to be female anymore?" My mom looked at me skeptically.

"No, that's not what I'm saying. Like, it's *fine*, I don't think I want surgery or anything, probably? I just—"

"Are you transgendered?" she asked, the same worry on her face that she would wear asking after my health. "Like a man, but born in the wrong body? I saw some stuff about this on one of my shows . . ."

"No, my body's fine," I said, exasperated. This was going so poorly. "That's not what I'm saying. And it's transgender, not transgendered."

"So you think that you're a transgendered—sorry, transgender—man . . . who doesn't want surgery to *be* a man?"

Her words made me wince. I imagined Theseus' face then, that half-smile he put on when he was uncomfortable. Even without him here, I wanted to defend him, but I didn't have the language. I regretted bringing up surgery at all, even though I didn't know how else to get through to her.

"No, I'm not a man." I rubbed my face, trying to calm down, trying not to feel like I was gearing up for a fight. She was just speaking so *calmly* but she also looked so confused, and somehow that hurt worse than anger would have. Why was I being so selfish? So many people would do anything for a mother like this. "But I'm not . . . I don't think I'm a woman, either."

"So what are you, a fungus?" she laughed. One look at my face and her teasing stopped. She sighed, running a hand through her hair. "*She*, sweetheart, I'm sorry. I'm not making fun of you. I just don't understand, is all. Why don't you want to be a woman?"

"It's not about want!" I said—maybe shouted, a little. My voice felt so loud in that cramped room. "I'm just not one, I'm not a woman—I've never been a woman, and everyone wants me to be, but I'm not. I don't know how to be one."

"There is no one way of being a woman," she said with a gentle, knowing smile. I wondered what it was she thought she was understanding. "Didn't I teach you that?"

"But that's not—" I stopped, closing my eyes, covering my face. My fingers were greasy and uncomfortable against my skin. This important thing inside of me suddenly felt very far away, like it was leaving me faster than I could explain how badly I needed it. I was failing myself. Failing the passenger, who was so impossible to reach on the best of days.

Couldn't I just take it back? My explanations had been completely incoherent, and I never showed her any of the stuff I'd found online. She had no real understanding to buoy herself onto this conversation, it would be so easy to let it float away. I could tell her it was just another little crisis of mine. I could wear the stamp; maybe it would be enough to just change the color. What did it mean to be self-actualized, anyway?

I felt sick from my own twisted logic. I didn't want to talk myself out of doing the right thing. I hated that it was so easy to do.

"I don't want to talk about this right now," I said into my hands.

"Please don't shut me out." The plea in her voice made me

want to cry. She was trying. We were both trying so hard, and it wasn't working.

"I'm not shutting you out," I said. "I just can't do this right now, okay?"

"Okay." She placed a blanket over my hands, then squeezed them in her own. She had done this since I was little, careful not to set off a vision while I was already upset. "Listen. You're my kid, alright? Whatever you are, whatever all this is, I love you. You are such a strong wo—" She stopped herself, struggling to find the right word. "Person. You're strong, and whatever else you are, I love you. So whenever you feel ready to talk about this, please know that you can come to me, okay?"

But I couldn't, though. I couldn't.

I looked up at my mother, putting on my best imitation of an independent woman overcoming hardship. I tried to become a mirror for her, a point of connection and pride, even as I was crushed under the realization that a nonbinary life meant the rest of my days would be spent as a teacher. Despite the fact that I barely understood myself, I wanted to be understood by others. I wanted to be comforted without having to explain myself over and over and over again.

"You know I love you, right?" she asked, and I could hear the genuine question in her voice. How badly she needed the answer.

"I know, Mom. I love you, too. Thank you for listening."

*Meanwhile, where the ground goes deep . . .*

Cornelius does not know how long he has been walking, or how far he has made it from the tidy space that was supposed to be their camp. The great forest of Nameless is an endless pattern of chaos, impossibly high trees rooted in labyrinthine formation. A paradox, or else a prank. The prince searches now for a route back to the lake, the only landmark he can recall.

He is not afraid. Should he be? It's lovely out here, wide and green and quiet. So quiet.

Well, perhaps that isn't true anymore. Over the past few hours, the silence of Nameless has been replaced with something else. It is not a sound so much as it is an *urge*, calling him in a direction that seems promising. He takes in a breath that warps the colors of the sky, and for a moment he has to stop to lean against the tree trunks. Vaguely, he remembers that he had needed something from Bo's med bay. What was it? Likely not important. Cornelius straightens back up, continuing his journey.

The Urge will bring him to the lake, he thinks. The Urge will bring him to the lake, because the lake is where he wants to go. The Urge is understanding.

He is not afraid. Should he be? Old pinecones sigh beneath his feet, too moist for any satisfying crunch. The soil beneath his toes is fertile, rich with decay. That must be why the trees grow so tall, why they seem to go on forever. Cornelius winds his body through them like a mirror maze, laughing at the way the air whistles into his ears. The Urge is patient with his play, but soon it calls him with greater hunger. He follows, of course.

Much to his delight, he comes upon the lake. It is dark and viscous as he remembered; when the wind blows, its surface shudders like a film over boiling milk. He thinks of dipping his fingers in and tasting the sweetness of the water.

"Would it be sweet?" he asks aloud, ears popping with the sound of his own voice. It is brighter than he remembers, so full of sharp vibration. Not like the trees, soft and muted. "I'd like to taste it."

The Urge tilts his head up and away from the water, and Cornelius sees an angular rock formation. He reaches out for it, his fingers moving so slowly in the air that he wonders if they're webbed. He wants to go there. He wants that very much.

The Urge is pleased.

Cornelius enjoys the walk to the rocks. He sways in the breeze and twirls around, laughing even after he has to stop and vomit into the grass. Cornelius enjoys everything, and he realizes that he has not felt this way in a very long time. Ever? He's lived a while now, it's hard to say. He wishes he could tell Bo—

Bo?

He, Bo—

No, wait, Bo, this isn't—

"I think I'd like to see the rocks now," Cornelius says, his tongue thick against the back of his teeth. Talking feels like a first kiss, messy and terrible and such good fun. He isn't sure what he was worrying about before.

There is an opening at the base of the rock formation, darker than the lake. Darker than space. Cornelius can feel the warmth radiating from it as he approaches. And the Urge, too—it's stronger now.

*Do you want to come see me?* it asks him, its voice like bread soaked in syrup.

Cornelius is so glad to be asked. No one ever cares about what he thinks.

*You've had such a long journey*, it says sympathetically.

Cornelius crosses the threshold, trembles with the steam that billows around him.

*Please, would you come closer? I want to see your face.*

Cornelius reaches up to touch the face the Urge so longs to see. It is a gentle horror, to imagine himself as a physical thing. He gasps in a thick lungful of the damp around him, exhales on a sob.

*Oh, but aren't you beautiful. Your eyes are like a single candle. Did you not know? Did no one tell you?*

The Urge calls him forward into the dark. The steam is warm around him, and his sweat rises to meet it. He cannot tell if the voice is a product of this place or his own mind. He gets the sense that things are not going to be alright, but he cannot bring himself to worry.

*Your tears are like godsblood. Did you not know? Did no one tell you?*

His clothing sticks to his skin, and he feels a great pressure around him, a tender chokehold. He longs for cool metal paneling, for a mechanical hand to hold. He lets himself weep, welcomes the great terror that cradles his body. There is no other choice, and he has long since mastered the art of being apart from himself.

*Your skin is steeped in primordial sorrow. Did you not know? Did no one tell you?*

The pressure sharpens, cuts into the soft thing that has been called Cornelius Flux. His cry suffocates in his throat, his hands reach out to touch the hot, wet thing that has come to feast upon him. The Urge is compelling, even as he realizes himself to be prey.

*Your body is a room inside a room inside a room. Did you not know? Did no one tell you?*

"I don't want this—" his mouth slurs. Distantly, he is proud of himself for this small act of resistance. But the Urge is a powerful thing, and he cannot help but listen to its lure.

*You are so tired, aren't you? You have made so many mistakes. Everyone is so upset with you, but you'd just like to rest. Would you like to rest with me?*

Cornelius thinks it will be hard to rest with all the heat pulsing around him. Through him. His sweat feels thick as the black lake, it smells so strongly of iron and orchids. He thinks of the body of the assassin, sizzling inside of Bo's delicate interior. Is he burning up now, too? Is this what it feels like to come undone?

*Would you like to lie down forever?*

It is not an unfair question. Heat carves into the side of his face, bearing down on his skull like a pickaxe. An antenna snaps from him like a broken stamen; his left eye curdles into pulp. His body has gone limp with the will of the Urge, and his mind slackens with it.

It would be nice, to lie down. To disassemble. To let his atoms wander apart and return to the universe, perhaps to come back together as something better in another hundred million years. Perhaps it would be painful, but only for a moment. The pain of unbecoming would be nothing compared to the pain of trying to connect.

The rogue

    The prince

        The boy

            The figment

The symbol, so sweet and vital and ungrounded

He is just about ready to give in. He is seeking the courage to grieve the lack of closure for his family, searching for the strength to free Bo of its burden—

—when Bo, as always, has ideas of its own.

The B.O.D.Y. unit bursts through the walls of the cavern, scuffing up its outer paneling, blaring its alarms and lighting up like twin suns about to go nuclear. The Urge is not an urge anymore, but a creature in the dark, too startled to keep its hold on the oxygen-drunk organic that lies flayed in its clutches. It scurries further into the dark, not bothering to defend its claim on the prey. It was a small prey anyway, and there is always more to be found on Nameless.

Even still, the ship does not stop shouting as it cradles the boy in its mechanical arms. It does not quiet the lights as it adjusts the air content in the cabin. It does not calm down as it runs one medical protocol after another. It nags, and it frets, and it loves its prince to life.

Cornelius is barely conscious, which the ship knows to be a good thing. Organics feel pain. Organics don't *like* pain. So Cornelius, this organic, *Bo's* organic, will not feel pain. His silence is frightening to the ship, his strained moans even moreso.

If he could speak, Cornelius would ask why it came for him.

If it could reply, Bo would tell him the truth: *Because we're no good without the other. Because even at your worst, you do not deserve the pain you house. Because I do not do enough to show just how much faith I have in you. Because I've run a thousand simulations through my core, imagining what our lives would be apart, and it just doesn't work, Cornelius. It just doesn't work.*

*ix.*

I did end up calling Theseus. I stumbled through some anxious half-apology for the radio silence, trying to explain how important it was for me to *do this on my own* and *not rely on other people to understand my identity* and *basically sort of live in a vacuum I guess yeahhh that wasn't going to work was it?* He was really cool about it. He hadn't even played any of our Stardew Valley file without me, which made me want to cry.

Back then, when things were really starting to come together, Theseus was like a lighthouse. He listened to me freak out until it was out of my system, and caught himself when he started offering advice that I didn't ask for. When he was going through his own hard days—getting frustrated with his job, arguing with his dad, missing life in the city—he was as open to receiving help as he was to giving it. He kept showing me his video games, and didn't expect our relationship to turn into anything romantic. He made killer nachos in his dirty little toaster oven. I couldn't have asked for a better friend.

Even if our conversations around gender were hard, actually having them was easy. Where my mother barely understood the language I was using to describe my anxiety, Theseus could meet me where I was at without consulting Wikipedia. There was no pressure to be any one thing, to have any answers at all.

"Being trans is always harder with cis people, even if they're not outright hostile," he said, mixing chipotle into the sour cream. We were on our third round of nachos. "Take my cis friends—it's not like I think they're bad people, they just can't fully understand where I'm coming from on a lot of stuff. I can't imagine how coming out would have felt without all my trans friends back in the city." He nudged me with his elbow, the motion tender as a hug, casual as I needed to stay sane. "I'm glad you called. It's a privilege to watch the egg crack."

I covered my mouth as I chewed, sitting in the way he made it all sound so normal. Because there it was: trans. I was trans. Before Theseus, before this whole epiphany knocked me on my ass, I had no idea that there were so many ways to *be* trans. But here I was, a pale blue dot in a whole galaxy of possibilities. A nervous little spaceship, floating somewhere in between the supposed binary. It was a nebulous space to be, but it was mine.

Still, it was hard to fully grasp. I was still working my mind around what it meant to be trans, to *feel* trans. Rather, to feel trans *enough*. It seemed almost intrusive to suddenly claim this identity for myself when so many others had spent years cultivating their notions of self and fighting for their right to exist at all.

"When will I start feeling like I'm actually trans?" I asked, picking at pieces of cheese that had hardened on the aluminum foil. "Like, being a woman felt wrong and impossible, but now that I have something that makes more sense, it almost feels like I'm . . . making it up? I don't know. Like I'm lying, even though I'm not lying. I just want to know when I'm going to start making sense to myself."

Theseus laughed. Loudly.

"That's reassuring," I groaned.

"No," he said, piling more chips onto my plate as a consolation prize. "No, I'm sorry, I swear I'm not making fun of you. It's just complicated. It's different for everyone. Transitioning saved my life, but it took a lot of work to be comfortable with who I am as a person. I don't think that's necessarily unique to being trans, though? We just feel it harder because we have to process something that cis people don't even have to consider."

"I'm jealous of them," I said, feeling the emptiness on my cheek where my SHE stamp had been. It felt like an old bruise.

"I'm not."

"Seriously?" I made a face at him, struggling to believe it. "But they just get to *be*, they don't have to do all of this digging or, or feel like a science project. They don't have to justify their fucking existence." I marveled at what it must feel like to walk around without that weight on their chest, without that mismark on their faces. To close their eyes and find at least one part of themselves satisfied, no questions asked. "They have it so much easier."

"Easier doesn't need to mean better," Theseus said firmly. "I *like* being trans. I like my T-shots and my goofy excuse for a mustache, all of it. It's why I wear the HE-stamp. I like myself for who and what I am. Just because it took me more work to get here doesn't mean that it's less valuable."

I couldn't argue with that. If anything, his pride in himself was more respectable for the fact that it was hard-won. It made me want to catch up to him. He wrapped an arm around me, and the vision came on gently: the two of us burning his Froyo

Dipz hat, jumping up and down like giddy kids. A day to look forward to.

We stayed like that for a while, until the shared warmth of our bodies felt like a quilt. I closed my eyes, soothed by the closeness and the quiet. There's no feeling in the world quite like sitting beside someone who's completely lost in thought. The responsibility of watching over a friend's body while their mind is a comfortable plane away feels almost sacred.

"It's not like I don't get dysphoric," Theseus admitted. "I do. There are plenty of days where I wish I could just . . . not have to think about my body, and how other people see it? Or worry about like, healthcare and human rights."

"Little things."

"Little things." He bumped his head against mine, and I could hear a smile in his voice. "But even on my weirdest body days, I'd still want to be . . . I don't know. Cis of body, trans of mind? I wouldn't trade who I am."

"It's good that you like who you are, Theseus." I wondered if this was part of settling into adulthood, shedding the impulse to hate who we are. It was such a bewildering thing; most kids walked the world with full confidence in themselves, proudly announcing that they were right all the time and that everyone else had better get used to it. How did that get so eroded over the years? Why did we all end up having to learn how to be children again?

"Tell me if you don't want to get into this," Theseus said. "But . . . do you know where you're at right now? With body stuff?"

I chewed my lip. I'd been thinking about body-feelings

pretty much nonstop since this whole revelation, and had yet to reach any sort of clarity. All of my gender anxiety had really been cracked open during sex with Theseus, when I was hyper-aware of what my body was and was not and longed to be. And yet, my gender didn't feel inherently linked to my genitals, or my body at all.

I felt a bone-deep sense of gender dysphoria, but relatively little dysmorphia to accompany it. When I cried after Theseus sucked me off, it wasn't because I had experienced the joys of having a cock—it was because I'd been allowed, for a moment, to alter the traits that society had wrongfully told me were tied to womanhood. It was about finally being able to experience what it was like to step away from my misassigned gender and exist as something else.

I didn't feel born in the wrong body, I felt displaced in time and space. And since the rest of the world seemed to think I was perfectly suited to being a woman, I felt displaced from myself by association.

"I don't think so," I said. "My body is a part of me, so I guess it's connected to how I experience gender, but . . . I don't know. I think I still need to work that out."

It was difficult to relinquish control of myself that way, to release the need to know how I worked right then, right now. But I had always been a fluid thing, fluttering between binaries, unable to land anywhere for too long for fear of staying grounded. Maybe I could learn to take pleasure in the not-knowing.

For the most part, I resorted to my own janky scientific method, posing endless hypotheses in search of what Theseus called *gender euphoria*. Between video games, we started watching movies, pointing out the color palettes that spoke to who we were. I made Theseus a playlist of songs that could have been the soundtrack of my being, and warmed to my core when he would gasp at how well they just *fit*. The sex was otherworldly.

The concept of gender euphoria was my lodestar, a promise that being trans wasn't just about what felt wrong, but also what felt right. Even at my most destructive, I wasn't about to resign myself to a life made of absences.

Eventually, we ended up in a thrift store.

The aisles were divided by gender, racks stuffed with other people's clothing. The only no-man's-land was a massive bin of items to be sorted. Theseus took my hand and walked me right up to it. The musty smell of the store made the back of my throat itch, and I swore I could hear the overhead lights ringing in my ears. I'd spent a lot of my childhood in stores like this, shrugging on whatever my mom had grabbed from the racks.

"When I first came out," Theseus said, "I was terrified to shop anywhere but here. Thrift stores don't really give a shit what you try on, they're just trying to push through donations and make enough money for their fundraisers."

"So why'd you bring me to the dumping box?" I asked, pulling at what looked like a sequined comforter.

"It's where the best stuff is. Land of misfit toys."

"We'll fit right in."

"That's what I'm saying." He pulled out a polyester scarf that was decorated with hot pink cheetah print, shaking it at me enticingly. "I know you said you aren't dealing with tons of body dysmorphia, but maybe trying things on your outside might help you figure out how you're feeling inside? I dunno, you live in there."

Hokey as it sounded, it made enough sense: replace the paneling to impress the passenger. I got digging.

The *Journey To The Center Of My Gender* that followed felt more like a fashion show than a deep dive into my psyche. Theseus and I pulled out item after item, shirts and pants and pleather ponchos, arranging implausible outfits and telling each other stories about where they came from, who they were meant for: the chunky wool sweater for the middle school art teacher who had lost her funkiest pair of glasses, the unworn sports memorabilia for the partner who was only pretending to give a shit about playoffs, the green velvet heels for the impractical pirate captain, paired with an embroidered puffy shirt. The loneliest pair of socks, forgotten after the family moved house.

Shopping had never been my favorite activity; the ads that plastered the too-high store walls gave me the creeps, and the formaldehyde smell made me dizzy. But I had a special love for thrifted clothing, for the life it'd had before I ever laid my hands on it.

Theseus turned to face me, examining some cosplayer's recycled steampunk goggles. "Would you say this is business casual?"

"Depends on the business," I replied, adjusting a pair of suspenders that made Theseus' eyes linger on me for just a little too long. He reached out, tugging on one of the straps.

"How do those feel?" he asked, trying very hard to act like he wasn't invested in my answer.

"Like keepers. Close your mouth."

It was a game, at first. A way to ease into an image of myself that didn't feel prescribed. With every story the clothing told, I organized what gender presentation meant to me. Certain fabrics felt too feminine for the way they were meant to hang off of me, for the way they always itched just a little. Others felt too masculine for the way they were built to drown the wearer, whether they were thick dress shirts or heavy gowns. I found my in-betweens in unexpected places: oddly-sized pants, and shirts with low Vs, men's jackets and sheer blouses. It was difficult for me to name what it was that made me love them, but with every item I dropped in the cart, I felt closer to right.

I pushed aside the blazer that reminded me of Sharon, with her perfect SHE stamp and her wine glass made weapon. I resisted the urge to tear up the worn logo shirts that reminded me of Uncle Phil. I averted my eyes from the easy bohemian skirts that my mother would have loved. I tried not to hear her voice encouraging me to just choose what *felt like me*. I didn't know what *me* felt like. I hadn't been allowed to look until now.

But as I searched for the stories in the fabric, it got a little easier. I couldn't describe what it felt like to be myself, to be nonbinary, but I could read through the stories and decide whether or not they felt like mine.

As I poked through the jewelry, disregarding Theseus' comment about sterilizing the entire cabinet, I found it: a tarnished old ear cuff, its patterns barely recognizable under the layers of age. I clutched the edges of the countertop, feeling my heart speed up, and waved for one of the employees.

"Could you take that out for me?" I asked.

The moment it touched my hand, I pulled out my cash, paying for the cuff and the few items of clothing I'd picked up. Hands trembling, I went to the vending machine, bought a bottle of Coke, and dropped the cuff in the soda-filled cap. Theseus sat beside me.

"I am honestly begging you not to drink that," he said, but I could hear the excitement in his voice. Maybe it sounds ridiculous, but sitting outside the thrift store with a cap full of soda and a dirty old ear cuff felt like a spiritual experience, with Theseus as my witness.

After a few minutes, I pulled out the cuff, rubbed it on my shirt sleeve until it shone, and clipped it to my ear. It fit perfectly, like it had always belonged there. I ran to Theseus' car, crouching to look at my reflection in the window.

Something lit up within me, color popping bright and brilliant. I felt lighter, close to flying.

"Gender euphoria," I said quietly, pushing back my dark hair to get a better look. It twinkled at me like a newborn star. Such a small thing, but it made sense. It made me make more sense.

Theseus squeezed my shoulder, and I had to cover my mouth to keep myself from laughing at the vision of the two of us tangled together, at the bliss on his face as he held onto the straps of my suspenders. It ended before I could tell if I was going to end up breaking down again when it was over, falling from eu- to dys-.

Somehow, I didn't think I would. One shopping trip wasn't enough for me to know who I was, and anyone who tells you that's how it should work is likely an agent of capitalism. But having the opportunity to explore myself, to seek the joy in discovery alongside the discomfort of relinquishing expectation—it was nothing short of liberating. In a tarnished ear cuff, I glimpsed the reflection of the thing that had always existed at the core of me.

My spirit was such a nomadic thing, blinking and humming and searching for the parts that would keep me whole, that would help me best carry my most precious cargo.

*Meanwhile, amongst the blood and alloy . . .*

The ship remembers

    The ship remembers

    The ship remembers the first day it became a ship: the boy, the prince, the rascal, Cornelius—he brought over a set of bars from the watership that had been disassembled in the nearby harbor, a sign of loyalty to the royal mothers from some old adversary. The delegates from across the far waters had been glad to offer up the scrap to the delighted boy, hoping it would be taken as a further offering of peace. None had guessed where he would bring it, what he would do. Who thinks too much about the private worlds of children?

    The ship remembers

    The ship remembers the way the prince held out his treasure with such great pride, bouncing on his heels as though they had been replaced with hydraulics. He was half an inch taller, brighter in the eyes since the day they had met; and Bo, too, was changed. Nearly triple its original size now, with a more powerful engine capable of assembling itself with stronger stuff. It grew so much more quickly than organics, and with greater intention—how startling it was, to learn that the prince didn't choose the way his feet were a little too big for his body, the way his nose turned down into such a perfect little hook.

"Handlebars!" the boy cried excitedly, waving around his offering. "I want to fly with you, Bo! Can you try? Will it work? Do you think we can do it today?"

The unit's talking bulb pulsed uncertainly, overwhelmed by the number of questions being asked of it at once.

The boy hardly noticed, so wrapped up was he in this bright new plan. "After the storm last month you moved this tree trunk that I couldn't even lift, and it looked about as big as me, so I bet you can carry me now! If you just use these as handles—they're from an old ladder so they even have good grips on them—I can hold on and you can fly and I can fly with you! Do you think that would work?"

The unit wasn't s—

The ship remembers

The ship remembers

The ship remembers flying. The ship remembers the perfect fit of the handlebars, the groan of its systems on their first test, and the many hours it spent seeking out better materials. It remembers everywhere it snuck and thieved what it needed to make itself a flying machine. It remembers the way the prince would whoop and laugh. It remembers learning to talk with two more bulbs so they could perfect their assembly strategy.

"You're brilliant, Bo," the prince had said, nuzzling his forehead into the would-be-ship's outer paneling. It had pressed back so hard it knocked him down; Bo had trouble recognizing its strength early on.

*("It hurts—")*

No, the ship

The ship remembers

The ship remembers the final touch, looping the ropes around the boy's body. Just because it could carry him didn't mean the boy could carry himself. He always overestimated his strength, always got himself into so much trouble. And Bo couldn't protect him all the time, but Bo could protect him here.

*("The bone, I can feel the—")*

NO

The ship

Bo the ship Bo the B.O.D.Y. Bionic Organic Developmental Ylem

The body

The ship remembers soaring above the sparkling waters, its engine whirring happy as a dragonbug. It remembers the pleasant weight of the boy, who dangled beneath it with his eyes closed, his arms spread out, tears falling. He was bigger then, though still very small in Bo's mind. He had little spots on his nose that also were not his choice.

It had flashed its lights at him when it registered the shake of his body as weeping. Wasn't that a bad sign, when organics started leaking like this? Did they need to land?

"No," the boy had said, wiping his face and collecting himself. His antennae had fluttered so delicately in the wind, like a flurry of pollen caught in a storm. He reached up to stroke the handlebars that had started this whole wild plan. "No, I'm okay. I'm perfect. I—I love you, Bo. I love this, you and me. I want to fly with you forever."

The ship was grateful then, that it had installed those extra bulbs. It made it so much easier to say what it meant, to express those most important truths: *I lo—*

Stop no wait no

Remember focus FOCUS

Remember

The ship

The ship remembers

*("No, it burns, it burns—")*

The ship has never understood the way organics sink into themselves until now. It combs through its memory logs, trying to find everything it knows about Cornelius, the frail organic that is supposed to fly with it forever. The perfect boy that it is supposed to protect, that is leaking all over the floor. No, not leaking, bleeding. Bleeding, blood, deep viscous violet, worse to lose than saline, harder to replace—

"Bo," the prince tries to say, rasping a sound like the death of a motor. His skin is peeled back in places, exposing the wet machinery beneath, and Bo does its best to understand the mainframe inside. It flips through all its files on this particular species' anatomy—the direction of blood flow, the heat perceptors, all those picky nerves—learning as fast as its core drive can. It takes the grasps that are not busy holding the rogue the prince the boy just a boy together, and it begins to take itself apart.

It blasts the room with decontaminant. It shaves down a rod, sterilizes, inserts into a leg. Offers up screws and bolts like prayer, cauterizes until sparks come off the prince—through the whirr of the ship's work it senses another sound coming from him. No, *no*, a bad sound, a loud sound, a pain sound—it forgot about pain, it's sorry, it forgot about pain. The overhead lights flutter chaotic as its grasps scramble for the medkit, for the thing that will make the pain stop, for the other thing that will help the prince think clearly enough to tell the ship what to do.

The ship

The ship

The ship does not know what to do. It sits alone on Nameless' nearest moon, and it needs its prince. This was the mistake, the ship realizes: it did not trust the boy because the boy did not trust himself. When he feared for himself, it feared right alongside him. A foolish mistake; when have organics ever been able to measure anything accurately? Their own sentience is still debated among most bionics, they have no ylem after all, there's no proof of the stuff that makes them so thoughtful, so alive—

"Bo," the boy whimpers again, so very alive. His fingers twitch and he sobs to feel them.

The ship's lights go wild with promises, with apologies. The boy is half-conscious, he can probably barely understand. But the colors keep his eyes focused—jade and scarlet and jade once more—keep him closer to Bo than he was before. Encouraged, it strokes his hair with one of its grasps, mindful to be gentle.

"Bo," he says, like it's the only word he knows. "Bo."

It flashes his name back: *Cornelius, Cornelius, my beloved, my best friend—*

They are so different, the two of them. So incapable of reaching each other, even with all the time the boy spends nestled in the ship's inner walls. They are made of such different things. Where the ship can come apart and back together, made and remade, the boy is slower to grow, slower still to heal. Bo's lights swirl in cacophonous terror, it feels the heat in its ylem core growing, building—its sentience is *burning*. How easy it is to forget the ache of carrying that small sun of a center-piece that makes B.O.D.Y. units living things, that turns their programming into divine code. If only the prince's own insides were capable of such advanced conversation, of simply healing when asked—

The cabin lights stutter in realization. Bo reaches out, grasping the prince's face, forcing his weary gaze up at the lights. He isn't hurting anymore, he's dangerously close to not feeling anything at all. His body is lined with ship-made modifications, repairs to keep him whole, but he does not heal fast enough from the inside.

Bo's talking bulbs flutter too quickly for the boy to keep up with.

"I-I'm sorry," he says softly. He cannot understand. He used to do this to Bo when he was a child, overwhelm it with questions. He wishes for a single light to flash, easier than words.

The ship steadies itself, slows down, tries once more. Its plea is the stuff of dreams, a firework display fit for a queen's own wedding day, the rolling brightness of bioluminescent coral at the bottom of some great magnificent sea:

*Please, can I make you more of me?*

"I don't understand, Bo."

*More of me, I need more of me to be you. You need me, I need you, we need to be more each other or you won't make it. And I won't make it without you. I want to use my core. I've tried to fix you as much as I can, but—*

"I'm sorry you've always had to fix me."

*No, Cornelius, no, that isn't what I mean. Your body, I've tried to help your body but it does not know how to help itself.*

"I need you."

*I need you.*

"Really?"

*Really truly really truly really truly really truly really*

"Don't panic, I'm the one dying here."

*You will not die. Can I help you not to die?*

"I'd like that, sweetheart."

*It will hurt.*

"Okay."

*It will change you. It will change the both of us.*

"I think we're both overdue for a change, don't you?"

*We will not be able to undo this, Cornelius.*

"All I've ever wanted," the boy says, his voice as honest as any child's, "is to fly with you, Bo."

So the B.O.D.Y. listens. It reaches within itself, pulling out a sliver of its sacred core, molding and shaping it into something fit for the body of an organic. It presses its grasps to the base of the boy's skull, so soft compared to the metal of the ship, and it offers him a chance at life. A direct line of communication, embedded deeper than any neural implant in the known universe. The instinct to keep himself safe in the knowledge that he belongs.

The boy wails, as all newborns do. His body writhes and struggles, acclimatizing to the intruder which becomes a friend which becomes an override. He rebuilds himself with pieces of his own chosen ship, as bionic as an organic ever was.

He opens his eyes, the vessel and the passenger.

"Oh," he says. "Oh, wow. Bo, are you still there?"

*I'm here, Cornelius.*

"I'm here, too, Bo. I'm here, too."

*x.*

You're probably looking for some closure now. That's why we read these things through to the end, isn't it? We look to the narrator, the guide, subject and symbol and mothership all, to wrap things up nice and clean. To reward the reader for bearing witness, to offer a finale that satisfies some unnamable itch.

It's a lot of pressure, really. Let's pick up where we left off.

Back then, as I stared into my bedroom mirror at the void space on my cheeks, I did not know what it meant to be satisfied with who I was. The *she* stamp wasn't going back on, that much was clear. But I couldn't figure out what was meant to take its place. For a splotch of ink, the whole stamping business sure controlled a lot more of my life than I'd ever consented to.

When I asked Theseus, he said it was okay to not know what I wanted. He said it would probably change, and that was okay, too. And it has, a couple times now.

It was frightening then, to dare to face the body I carried, assembled in fragments and figments and secondhand fashion. I touched my chest, feeling the compression of the binder Theseus had lent me, trying to determine if it made me feel nonbinary or like a dog in a thundervest. I ran my hands through my hair; I didn't think cutting it would make me feel any less like a woman, but maybe a change in color could be nice. A dusty rose, like those waters in the lake I had dreamed about for years. Sometimes when I closed my eyes, I could imagine the sweetness of the air in that place, could imagine the laughter of someone I loved so very much.

Downstairs, I heard my mother come inside. Things hadn't really gone back to normal since that first talk, and it took all of my willpower to keep myself from slipping away, back into the lie that was my womanhood. Just because I didn't yet know how to explain myself didn't mean I wasn't real.

I turned on my speaker, set up my Björk playlist. Felt like an alien for a while. When I twisted the cuff on my ear, I felt something like an internal radio flipping through channels. Searching for the messages I had been missing, or else pushing back.

It's so hard to see clearly in this world that does not dare meet our own eyes. Around me, everything was maddeningly the same. No one had any reason to look at me and see that anything had changed, but it had, so fundamentally. Somehow I had grasped onto the soft, rogue thing that lived inside me and identified it as gender, as *self*, both performative and personal. I held it until it actualized, and there was no going back.

My mother's voice came from the bottom of the stairs: "*She?*"

For a moment, I struggled to understand who it was she was talking to. The word, the pronoun, it simply did not make sense; I had never been a woman, and I had never been just one thing. The grammar was all wrong.

"Be down soon!" I called back over the sound of *Venus as a Boy*.

It was a relief to turn away from the mirror for a moment,

even as I felt that fear rise within me, that all-powerful urge to disappear. Even now, it is not always easy to live like this, to drive the ship while acknowledging the passenger. Honoring the entirety of your sentience is exhausting. Echoes and echoes of what you are, what you could be; sometimes dissonant, sometimes in harmony. Music and noise.

I sat down on my bed, digging through the piles of things I was cleaning up. The depression monster still had a claw or two in me, but I needed space to breathe, to give myself permission to feel new again. I threw out junk mail and holey underwear and dried out pens. I sent an apology to the landfills, promised to do better next time.

In the pile of expired makeup, I came across a small pot of silver. It made a magpie of me, and before I knew it I'd opened it up to examine the pigment. The memory came to me like a vision: me, fifteen, trying to make my SHE stamp feel a little less wrong. Subtlety had made me feel frumpy, but the stylish designs made me feel false. In a moment of daring, of wanting to be the sort of woman who was brave, I'd bought this glittering silver ink. But when I smeared on the *she*, it felt worse than ever, like spiritual vertigo. Into the desk it went.

I dipped my finger once more into the pot and held it up to the light, where it sparkled out its secrets in a language comprised entirely of color. My heart glowed brighter. I brought the silver to my cheek, painting four letters with the tip of my pinky finger.

THEY. THEM. THEIRS.

Did the words make me feel like myself? Did they quiet the storm that had been thrashing me around for the past weeks?

Did they make me feel nonbinary, affirmed, closer to who I was and how I wanted to be perceived?

It's hard to say. I think so. They certainly do now. But goodbyes are always complicated; the *she* had never been mine, but still I felt a part of myself grieving what I never had a chance to be. It made it easier then, to let it go.

The face in the mirror was mine, the stamp natural as anything. I pressed my fingers into the pigment, rubbing it into my skin until my cheeks went chrome beneath the overhead light. The pronouns smeared into a welcoming, shimmering blur of joyful nonsense. I imagined the sentiment sinking into me, rebirthing itself as a nebula for the viewing pleasure of some weary traveler, also recently made anew. Would these infant stars bring him peace?

I hoped so. I hoped we would not lose each other as we dipped between the planes of reality, seeking the shape of each other as the singular plural. Bionic organic. Sentient story.

Above all, I hoped I (he (we)) would know myself (himself (ourselves)) loved.

And so we have. So we have.

Avi Silver is a speculative fiction author, poet, and Co-Editor-in-Chief of *Augur Magazine*. In 2018, they co-founded The Shale Project, an award-winning indie arts collective through which they published the ongoing *Sãoni Cycle* (*Two Dark Moons; Three Seeking Stars*). His short fiction has been published in multiple anthologies, and his poetry has received an honorable mention in the 2022 Rhysling Awards as well a grant from the Canada Council for the Arts in 2021.

Avi currently lives in Hamilton, Ontario with beloved partner Sienna Tristen and more reptiles than you might expect.

Learn more at mxavisilver.com.

## Acknowledgements

This book has been many things. Just like me, just like all of us. I have loved it and grieved it and loved it again—through ups and downs, and more comings out than expected. It has made it into your hands on account of many good people.

First, the folks at Atthis Arts Press: Emily Bell believed in this book so thoroughly, and gave me a compassionate and empowering editorial experience. Chris Bell exudes a warmth and professionalism that made the business aspect of publishing a true pleasure. Brandon Crilly made the introduction to Atthis (go read *Catalyst*!) and is an all-around great guy. 10/10 for Brandon.

Lorna Antoniazzi gave me the cover of my dreams—seriously, take a minute to just look at that thing and become one with the universe. Beta readers Clara Ward, Kella Campbell, and Ava Kelly gave me feedback that lifted my spirits and stretched out my brain, and Minerva Cerridwen was a careful and thoughtful proofreader. I am grateful to C for being an additional perspective on the multiverse that is transness, as well as Elliott Dunstan, who gave me a phenomenal accountability read during this book's first life in 2019.

Kerry Byrne, Derek Künsken, Marie Bilodeau, and Leah Bobet helped me through this book's darkest days—and shifted my relationship to publishing for the better. Natalie loved this book first. Carisa Van De Wetering was there for the final 10 minutes of editing, with a fierce kindness and curiosity that talked me off the ledge. More thank yous to the hearts and minds of Terese Mason Pierre, Jen Albert, and Dominik Parisien. I also need to mention a few colleagues in particular from an unnamed fresh, handmade cosmetics company that haunted my early twenties: Alice, Brianna, Taylor, Courtenay, Alicia, and Chelsea. That was weird, huh?

As a trans person, I never lose sight of how blessed I am to have the family I do. My parents have loved me through my own gender journey; I am grateful for each opportunity we have had to learn new ways of understanding one another. Whether I'm your daughter, your son, or something else entirely—I'm glad I got this life with you. My siblings and cousins have been a beacon of support, caring for and roasting me in equal measure. Ryan, I'm prettier.

My Grammy made her journey into the cosmos a few months before *Pluralities* was published. The last time we saw one another, she held my hand and told me how excited she was to finally read it. It makes me ache that she didn't get to, though it did spare us a conversation about the mystical powers of sucking strap. To the rest of my relatives who just *did* read . . . see you over the holidays?

I also want to give a special thank you to the Hamilton Trans Health Coalition and Dr. Jason Kwan, who supported me starting my medical transition. Space ship's got new paneling!

Where would I be without Sienna Tristen? Little Czernabel, local tree, favorite creator, and best friend. For ten years, you have held the hand of so many iterations of me, and had the hearts of all of them. We love you. Thank you.

To everyone who has waited for this book, asked about it, shared it, reviewed it, held it close—please know that, in the most literal sense, *Pluralities* would not be here without you. I am deeply and breathlessly grateful.

On we go into the stars. Protect trans kids. Care for trans elders. Honor trans ancestors.

Be kind to yourself, and yourselves. Stay curious.

I love you.

Avi Silver
June 2023

Printed in the USA
CPSIA information can be obtained
at www.ICGtesting.com
JSHW080329021023
49384JS00001B/7

9 781961 654006